ZOMBIES
AND
FAIRY TALES

AN UNDEAD ANTHOLOGY

ZOMBIES
AND
FAIRY TALES

AN UNDEAD ANTHOLOGY

EDITED BY
ANTHONY GIANGREGORIO

Copyright © 2012 Undead Press
ISBN Softcover ISBN 13: 978-1-61199-077-5
ISBN 10: 1-611990-77-7
For more info on obtaining additional copies of this book, go to:
www.undeadpress.com
Cover art by Shane Koch

Table of Contents

THE PRINCESS AND THE ZEE

R P STEEVES

All the wars, sieges and acts of terror she had witnessed from her cushioned throne could never prepare her for the savagery and horror that had befallen her kingdom at the hands—and jaws—of the Unliving Ones.

It all happened so quickly. The plague had swept through the village, but it was no ordinary pestilence of boils.

Normally, such an event resulted in a few months of misery, piles of bodies to be burned, and occasionally a decree from her father forbidding entry into the kingdom.

But this time it was...different, and far, far worse.

The bodies of villagers who had been stricken with fever and died in fiery, sweat-drenched agony had been collected as usual and piled in pits on the outskirts of town.

But rather than lying there to fester, growing bloated and rank and overridden by insects, the bodies had risen. But not like a miracle of resurrection, but instead in a twisted mockery of life.

One astute observer had opined that these deathless creatures marked the end of humanity, like the close of a play. They had then been dubbed 'Zees,' a term which had replaced far more offensive slang used by the roughest of individuals.

But naming them was one thing. Stopping them was another.

Their hunger, upon waking, was insatiable, and they devoured the people of the village in short order. Many more became infected by their presence.

No one quite knew how the plague was spread: by touch, through the air or something else, something that infected their very souls. Unfortunately, it took far too long to discover how the Zees could be killed for good. Destroying their heads seemed to do it, but that was easier said than done.

In the meantime, the creatures had overrun the village and stormed the castle. The enormous stone structure, which had stood up to countless attacks and sieges over the centuries, had not been a match for the mindless monsters.

The creatures had sloughed through the moat and climbed the walls, moving in a wave, a tide of undead that poured into the Queen's home, her bedchambers.

It was only through the sacrifice of her father, the King, and his loyal guardsmen that she had been able to escape through a secret tunnel.

That is how the Princess, known colloquially as Princess Larissa, came to be traveling through the wastelands with only the Fool and the Captain of the Royal Guard as her royal escort.

But you could hardly tell by looking at her that Larissa was indeed, a Princess. Her royal finery was long gone, and she wore the rough hides of the local wildebeests, skinned for her by the Captain. She was covered in grime, and more often than not, the blood and viscera of the Zees.

Her companions had not fared much better.

The Fool's hat covered in bells was long gone, as was his cane. His pants were discarded and, he too, wore the hides of the wildebeests. But he had replaced his lost trinkets with trophies taken from the fallen Zees slaughtered by the Captain.

He shook a twice-dead man's femur as if it was a rattle—he called it his 'rubber chicken' for some reason. If he had not been considered mad before this, then the insanity of the new world order had surely infected him. He wore a necklace of ears proudly, and rolled a pair of eyes in his hands while rhythmically humming.

Of the three, the Captain was the only one who seemed more or less unscathed. He still wore his armor. His helm was dented and dulled by battle, but it still protected his head.

His shield was a constant source of succor for Larissa, and his sword had fiercely protected the group from the mindless hordes of Zees that littered the land.

They had traveled across the kingdom through endless weeks of hiding, running and fighting, with precious little eating or sleeping. It was a far cry from the life of comfort and leisure to which Larissa was accustomed.

But the Captain had assured her that comfort would be hers once more at the end of their journey. They were headed for the nearest neighboring kingdom, the land of Critch, once the sworn enemy of her people, but now their only chance for survival.

And after a long, bloody trail, they were almost there.

If they survived one last encounter.

The Zees had snuck up on them. Even after all this time, the small band of misfits could still be taken unawares by the silent, methodical movements of the creatures.

They had crept out of the misty morning woods and attacked the group. Larissa herself had been on watch, but she had nodded off, and by the time she heard the breaking of a twig near her ear, there was a pair of snapping jaws only an inch from her face.

She screamed.

This roused the Captain and the Fool, who sprang from their slumbers and reacted. The Fool, useless as ever, merely commenced hooting and dancing about.

He would later claim that it was an attempt to distract the creatures, but the Zees had never once turned their attention from their prey when faced with his lunacy.

The Captain, though, was swifter and surer in his actions.

He sprung forth, his filthy blade whistling through the air, slicing one creature's head from its neck in a swift, sliding stroke.

The head toppled to the forest floor, as an explosion of blood and ichor blasted forth from its neck, drenching the Princess. She shrieked once more, as the second creature's rotted teeth caught her once-silken locks in an iron bite.

The Captain gripped her hair in one hand and sliced through it, eliciting another shriek from the Princess and a howl from the Fool. The Captain turned to chastise the jester and, in a moment of distraction and weakness exacerbated by fatigue and frustration, he took his attention off the Zee.

4

The monster grasped the Captain by the shoulders and sunk its teeth into his neck.

He could barely gasp as the blood fountained from the wound, and he dropped to his knees. The slick film of bodily fluids caused the Zee to lose its grip, and with the last of his strength, the captain put the tip of his blade through the left eye of the creature, the tip sticking out the back of its skull.

Then the two of them, dead and doubly dead, collapsed to the ground in a heap of death and foul excrement.

Larissa screamed once more and the Fool, shaking his thighbone rubber chicken, sidled over to the fallen creature, plucked out its remaining eye, and grabbed the Princess by her dainty hand. "Come with me if you want to live," he said, and led her off into the morning light.

By the time they arrived at the castle gate, it had become a dark and stormy night in the land of Critch.

The Fool and the Princess were drenched, their wildebeest cloaks matted and wet, their hair, skin and spirits soaked to the bone. But they had made it through the forest unscathed, and they were ready to beg for sanctuary at the home of their enemy.

The guard at the door was skeptical of their credentials, to say the least, but he let them in nonetheless. He must have decided to let someone of royal blood make the decision as to whether or not this ratty, disgusting woman was who she claimed to be.

"But I am the Princess Larissa of the Kingdom of Men," she proclaimed in her haughtiest voice.

Queen Rosalinda of the Kingdom of Critch was not convinced. "You appear to be nothing more than a filthy beggar, my dear," she stated plainly, her regal sweetness still intact, though it was clear to Larissa that the surrounding lands had been just as ravaged by Zees as her own kingdom. "Besides, my dear, not only can I not confirm your claim of royal blood, but I cannot even be sure that you and your…companion…" With this, Queen Rosalinda glared daggers at the Fool, dirtier and madder than ever, shaking his 'rubber chicken' at the shadows on the wall. "Are not, in fact, infected."

Then a young man next to the Queen leaned over from his throne to hers to whisper in her ear. He was tall and strong, fair-haired and clear-eyed.

The Prince of Critch, the man who would be Marcus the First, was a war hero. He had fought bravely in battle against The Kingdom of Men, and according to the bards who wandered the halls of the castle tuning their new songs, this Marcus of Critch had been a hero of the War of Zee as well.

There were few who knew more about the creatures than he, so when he spoke, his mother listened.

"There will be…a test," she proclaimed, with just a bit more regal inflection than necessary. "You shall be sequestered, and your jester…"

"Fool!" the Fool cried, his tongue hanging out of his mouth, his brown hair matted, his weak eyes squinting. The Queen ignored him.

"Your Fool shall sleep on your floor. If either of you develops The Sickness, you shall be killed immediately. But if you survive, then of course you shall be cleaned up, given the finest robes and shoes, and if it pleases you, you shall have the hand of my son, Marcus." The Queen smiled, though it was an inscrutable smile.

Larissa, for her part, was thrilled. Marcus was a far better match for her than her original mate, arranged by her father. That 'prince' (and he was such in title only), had been much like the Fool: small and scrawny, with weak eyes and far from fair of face. She would be better off with this heroic Prince.

If she survived the night.

She was given a bath and the finest perfumes, and fresh, clean silks to wear. She was then led up the winding stairs of the highest tower to a room unlike any she had ever seen.

On the floor was a bearskin rug. This is where the Fool would sleep, though ever since he had been cleaned up and dressed in new hose he had been extremely quiet, and had been mopping his brow the entire journey up the tower.

Prince Marcus had taken Larissa to his room personally, though he had been gentleman enough to leave her cleaning and primping to the female servants. Thankfully, he was there to explain the bizarre sleeping arrangements before her.

For, aside from the bearskin rug, the rest of the room was dominated by an enormous bed, and a multi-story ladder that one would need to mount it. The cavernous room was lit by one single oil lamp located on the stone floor.

"There are twenty mattresses here, and twenty box springs," Marcus explained, as if it was the most common arrangement in the world. "You'll sleep on top of that. If you survive the night, you shall prove to my mother that you are who you say you are. After that, well, it will only be a matter of time before you're mine." He broke into a wide grin and Larissa felt her heart flutter. "Trust me; our marital bed will be quite different from this one."

She swooned as he said this, and her breath caught in her throat. She was so swept up in the dream of bliss—and babies—with Marcus that Larissa scarcely noticed a hand close around her throat.

She gasped—or tried—as the fingers closed around her windpipe, then twisted her face to see her assailant. There, pressed up behind her, with wild red eyes, was The Fool.

He grasped his necklace of ears with one gray, dead hand, his eyes shining blood red.

He had been infected and had succumbed!

He was a Zee! And he was killing her.

But, thankfully, her knight in shining armor—only now he was resplendent in his finest silk tunic and breeches—leapt into action. He drew his short sword and severed the arm of the Zee that had once been the Fool. Blood spurted from the wound, sullying the new gown that Larissa now wore.

Then, in one strong slice, Marcus cleaved the undead Fool's head in half, and the Zee slumped to the floor. The prince stooped over the monstrous corpse and plucked out the creature's eye. Then, without a word, he rang the call bell, summoning the courtesans. Larissa would need to clean up once more.

She stretched out on the mattress, and for the life of her, couldn't get comfortable.

It was not, to her surprise, a matter of calming her mind. Yes, she was frightened and disturbed by the events of the past twelve hours, but she had been trapped in a world of constant fear for so long, that it was hardly a new experience.

Certainly she would miss the Fool and the Captain, but they had been nothing more than servants to her, and now she had a chance to marry Prince Marcus and start a new life.

Surely the Zee infestation would eventually be put down, and peace would return to the land.

No, it wasn't her mind that was causing her distress; it was the mattress beneath her.

But it wasn't as if the irritant was a singular lump in her back. She was used to that, of course. Those of royal birth like her were hypersensitive to such matters. Even an object as small as a pea under twenty mattresses and twenty box springs would cause her discomfort.

She could imagine Marcus placing something under the mattresses to test her. In fact, when the Queen had mentioned a test,

Larissa had half expected it to be this, and she thought she had spied Marcus fiddling around near the bed frame earlier.

But this was no lump. This was something…writhing.

It wriggled and moved underneath her, undulating and moving, slithering and sliding as she tried to relax.

She wasn't imagining it.

Then, after a seemingly interminable time, the movement changed. The mattress beneath her no longer writhed. Now, it *shook*.

She felt a steady, rhythmic pulsing beneath her. Something was pounding away at the mattresses, and the pounding was getting fiercer. More powerful.

She had never been afraid of the dark before, but now she was terrified. The sole light on the floor seemed leagues away.

She rose, and as she sat there sweating, the pounding ceased. She released the breath she didn't know she was holding. It was over. She had survived the test and could go to sleep.

Then, as she breathed out, she heard a horrible rending noise and the fabric around her began to rip.

Suddenly, two cold, strong hands erupted from the mattress on either side of her and pulled her downward.

She screamed the scream of the damned as a head tore through the fabric behind her, and she could hear chomping, slobbering jaws as they readied themselves to take a bite from her flesh.

But she would have none of it. She shook off the shock and acted, driving her elbow into the creature's jaw again and again. The monster couldn't feel pain, but it did react to momentum. It rocked backward, and using the leverage she had gained, she fought her way free of the thing's iron grip.

She scampered away from the Zee, which fought its way through the remaining mattress, as Larissa fled, horrified that the ladder had fallen away from the bed in the chaos. Gripped by fear, she lost her balance and tumbled off the side of the mountain of mattresses.

Vertigo snatched her stomach as she fell, and she reached out, grabbing hold of the top mattress and holding on for dear life. The creature moaned as it moved toward her. It would pull her up and devour her before she could even move. She would be dead, or even worse, become a mindless monster of hunger herself.

The Zee hovered over her, ready to take a bite from her fingers, which were tight and tired, barely holding on.

She pushed off with her feet, falling backward, and pulling as she fell. The massive pile of mattresses toppled to the earth and Larissa twisted her body in midair.

A moment later, she landed—not on the hard concrete floor, but on the massive pile of mattresses.

She was alive…and right next to the undead creature.

She wasn't out of danger. She had fallen from the frying pan into…

The fire.

She reached over, taking hold of the single oil lamp that lit the room, and touched the flame to the pile of mattresses. The dry straw that the mattresses were stuffed with ignited instantly and soon the entire room was filled with a cleansing blaze.

The Zee waved its arms fruitlessly. It too was ablaze.

Larissa turned and heaved the heavy wooden door open, then fled for the stairs.

"I am sorry to have put you through that, my dear, but we had to be sure about you." The Queen's voice was neutral once again, and her smile was as enigmatic as ever. "We have known for a long time that the creatures can infect you through their body parts, though royals are, by virtue of their blood, immune."

At least that explained what had happened to the Fool, Larissa thought.

"We also knew that, on occasion, the Zees can grow from discarded body parts. It was, of course, a calculated risk. If you did not turn in the night, you were surely a royal, and if you survived an attack by the creature, well, you would then be brave and resourceful enough to marry my son."

Marcus, for his part, was genuinely smiling. "I'm the one who placed the eyeball of your fool under the mattress, so if you must hate someone, hate me."

Larissa gazed at him, her hazel eyes full of nothing but love and visions of the future: blissful marriage and lots of royal babies. "I could never!" she cried.

"Good. It would not do for my wife to hate me. Especially now that the generals have informed us that the kingdom is now free of monsters. We have defeated them from A to Zee."

Larissa beamed and ran across the room into his arms. It seems that sometimes, dreams did come true and there was such a thing as a happy ending.

She was looking forward to living happily ever after.

ZOMBIELOCKS AND THE THREE BEARS

ANTHONY GIANGREGORIO

Once upon a time the dead began to walk.

"The dead are attacking the living," screamed the newspapers. "They're eating the flesh of their victims! Shooting them in the head is the only way to stop them!"

No, this wasn't a horror movie, it was real life.

Somehow, someway, the dead had begun to walk and were now feasting on the living. Weight Watchers was forever over and Jenny Craig had become a midnight snack for a horde of ghouls; now there was only the dead and the living, and the living were shrinking fast.

Goldie Patterson was seventeen and alone in the world, thanks to the dead eating her parents last night. Now she was on the run, didn't have a friend in the world, and had nowhere to go. The streets were dangerous, zombies everywhere, as well as roving packs of hoodlums who used the lawlessness as a chance to rape and pillage. To say it wasn't a good time to be beautiful and blonde was an understatement.

Goldie was beautiful and then some, with long gold locks and even longer legs, a full chest, and a slim waist—any boy in school would have chewed off their left leg to go out with her. Of course now, many of those boys had had their legs chewed off, only for an entirely different reason.

So far she'd only managed to survive being raped, killed or eaten—choose whatever order you prefer—by being sneaky and hiding, as well as making sure to keep her long gold tresses and curvaceous figure hidden. Her attire consisted of a hoodie with the hood pulled over her face and a pair of old denim jeans that would have been fashionable on a farmer and no one else. A pair of ratty sneakers filled out the list.

Knowing she had to get out of the city if there was even a chance in hell of surviving, she found a bicycle with blood on the seat and a severed hand still wrapped on the left handlebar, and began to ride out of the city—she left the severed hand on the ground behind her.

The going was rough and more often than not she had to leave the bicycle in the street and hide in the bushes or behind an abandoned car. Zombies were absolutely everywhere and more than once she almost didn't make it, as the ghouls surrounded her and tried to grab her. Teeth came close to her soft skin but never seemed to connect.

Believe it or not, her worst enemy was other humans. Once or twice men had seen that there was a sexy girl hiding under her clothes and had tried to grab her. What they would do to her was far worse than what any zombie would do.

Of course, the similarities were there. Both wanted to 'eat' her. Both wanted to force her to the ground and get on top of her. and both wanted to make her theirs.

It took her hours but eventually she reached the city limits. From there she weaved between the vehicle-choked highway until she was clear of the worst of the cars and trucks. She tried not to look at the bodies in the cars, most now having become zombies. She tried not to think about them, what it must feel like to be dead yet still living—so to speak. She didn't want to imagine still being able to think and be aware, to feel your body slowly rotting off your bones as it began to decay.

That night she found a gas station and hid behind it, between a dumpster and an old car with no tires and its windows shattered. She slept fitfully, and woke many times when cars sped by the gas station on their way to who knows where.

One time two cars pulled into the station; men got out and after breaking into the gas station, began ransacking it. Two hours later they drove off and Goldie was glad they were finally gone. She had been terrified that she would be discovered.

Finally, after a long night fraught with peril, the sun rose and she set off again.

She made it five miles before she got a flat and the bicycle became useless. Then she set out on foot, doing her best to keep to the shoulder of the road and hiding each time she heard a car coming.

She didn't know where to go, but when she spotted a sign for the nearby state forest, she figured that would be a good place to go. Still, she was starving and there was nothing to eat anywhere.

But then good fortune smiled on her when she came upon a car on the side of the road. Peering into one of the windows, she spotted a diaper bag on the seat. The bag was open, its contents having spilled out onto the seat, and clearly she could see powdered formula, baby food and two bottles of water.

Her mouth salivated at the thought of eating even that.

But then from the front seat a zombie popped up, slapping its face against the window and smearing blood and pus across the glass. Goldie jumped backwards, terrified, and then when she realized the zombie was trapped in the car, she became more brave and returned to the window.

She was now able to study the zombie, something she had never been able to do before when running from them. She could see the zombie was a woman and on further inspection realized that the woman was a mother, because looking past the face, she also spotted the car seat in the back seat beside the diaper bag. She had been so excited to see the food that she hadn't even seen the car seat beside it. In the car seat were the remains of a small body, only a torso left.

The bloody lips on the zombie told the fateful tale, how a mother had devoured her child after becoming one of the living dead.

Her stomach growling in sync with the zombie told Goldie that time for watching was over, and that if she wanted the baby food within the car, she would have to draw the zombie out and kill it.

Slowly her hand went to the car door to open it and then stopped before touching the handle. She needed a weapon, something to kill the zombie with. What was she thinking? Was she going to fight the zombie with only her hands? Of course not. She was tired and hungry and wasn't thinking clearly. She stepped away from the car and had a look around the area. At first there wasn't much she could use as a weapon but as she kept looking, she began to find things she could use. Her arsenal consisted of a fist-sized rock, dirt, and finally a two foot long tree branch that had broken off a tree in a storm and now was a suitable club.

She gathered everything about ten feet from the vehicle and then went back to the car door. At first she had second thoughts, not wanting to have to face the zombie, but then her stomach growled again and she knew she had no choice. With one quick look around at the empty road, she stepped up to the door, grabbed the handle, and pressed the button that would open the door.

Nothing happened. The door was locked. She let out the breath she was holding and seemed to deflate like a balloon as the adrenaline rush that filled her subsided slightly. She actually felt lightheaded as the endorphins suffused her system.

The zombie inside the car was going wild, slapping the window and smearing it with blood and mucous so that the glass became opaque. Goldie pulled herself up and then went around to the other side of the car, reached for the handle, and pulled it open. She had half-expected it to be locked too so when the door opened easily she was a little bit surprised.

But the zombie wasn't. Upon the zombie seeing it was free from its prison, the dead woman lunged across the seat and fell out of the car, her upper torso and head slamming hard onto the ground.

If Goldie had been quick and not afraid to attack, she could have possibly stepped on the zombie's head and done something to put the ghoul down right there. But instead, Goldie panicked, screamed, and ran away as the zombie pulled itself across the ground and began to rise.

Goldie ran away but after a few steps stopped and began moving in a circle so that the zombie was following her. The two began running around the car as if they were playing a game of tag, only Goldie was screaming for help.

On the third time around the car, and after Goldie realized that the zombie couldn't catch her, she began to calm down a little and also recalled that she had prepared weapons to kill the ghoul. When she was at the back of the car she then peeled off for her pile of stuff, and when she got there, she reached down and scooped up two handfuls of dirt, her hands pressed together to make a bowl. When the zombie came at her, Goldie was ready, and though she screamed and squeezed her eyes closed, she threw the dirt right at the dead woman's face.

The zombie was struck in the eyes and was blinded immediately. With no sight, the ghoul veered off its attack path and brushed by Goldie before stumbling to the ground.

Goldie opened her eyes to see the area in front of her empty, and when she heard moaning behind her, she turned to see the zombie on the ground, its hands wiping and brushing at its eyes like a wild animal. With limited intelligence, the dead woman didn't understand why she couldn't see.

Goldie picked up the fist-sized rock, sighted her target, and threw the rock as hard as she could at the zombie. The rock flew true and conked the dead woman on the head. Her head snapped back and then forward, and though there was a circular dent on its forehead, the ghoul appeared to be fine. Frowning, Goldie picked up the tree branch, and feeling brave now that the zombie couldn't see, she stepped up to the prone ghoul and began to whack the dead woman on the head.

The first blow didn't do much damage, but with each consecutive blow, the head began to take on the consistency of a rotten tomato. The brains began to seep out of the cracks in the skull and gore and blood that became stuck to the tree branch was flung off in all directions. By the time Goldie stopped, the head had been smashed into a dark-red paste.

Heaving from the exertion, she dropped the tree branch and plopped down on her butt, her entire body feeling as if she would explode. She'd just killed someone, and though technically the person was already dead, it still didn't deter her away from looking at the body before her with guilt.

Then her stomach grumbled, as it didn't have any qualms about becoming filled, despite the situation. So coming to her knees, she was careful not to touch any of the spilled brain matter as she stood up.

Going to the car, she tried not to look at the small and torn body in the baby seat. Reaching in quickly, she grabbed the diaper bag, the bottled water and baby food that had spilled out. With her hands full, she walked a few feet away, repacked the diaper bag and slung it over a shoulder, then continued walking down the road. She planned to stop and eat in a minute, but for now she wanted to get away from the scene of to what she felt was a murder.

She didn't give the small twinge of pain on her right arm a second's thought, assuming she had pulled something when she had beaten the zombie down, but unknown to her; there was a small bite mark there.

Earlier, one of the zombies had managed to bite her when she'd had to fight through them, and even now the infection was growing inside her.

Hours later, Goldie was on the move again. She'd made the formula and drank it greedily, then ate the baby food in the tiny jars, but as soon as she did this she vomited the entire contents up. She felt weak and dizzy and didn't know why.

But she continued moving, walking deeper into the forest.

Just before night she came across a small shack pressed up against the side of a mountain. With night falling, she had to go somewhere so after knocking and not finding anyone home, she let herself in and explored her new surroundings.

It was a quaint little home, with three rooms: the kitchen, a living room and a bedroom. In the bedroom were three beds, and each one was slightly bigger than the others, so that they were small, medium and large.

Goldie went to the first bed and tried it, but though she was exhausted and didn't feel well, she found the bed far too hard to sleep on. So she went to the second one and found it far too soft. But the small one was just right and she curled up on it and fell into a deep sleep, which quickly became a coma as the zombie infection inside her raged. She never regained consciousness as she lapsed into death.

Sometime later, a family of bears—Papa Bear, Mama Bear, and Baby Bear —arrived at their home, entered, and were shocked to find a human girl sleeping in their child's bed. Now, these bears weren't cuddly. Their fur was ragged from a hard winter, spots missing to let skin show through. Their faces were rough with a few healing wounds from battles in the forest with other bears, and their bones could be seen under their fur, their bodies lean from hunger. Times had been tough lately and it was all they could do to simply eke out a living and survive. So when they saw a human girl in one the beds, it was like an imaginary dinner bell had been rung.

"Who is she?" Papa Bear said to Mama Bear in bear talk as his stomach rumbled in hunger.

"I don't know, dear," Mama Bear said, "but I guess we don't have to worry about what we're going to have for dinner."

"Can I play with her first, Mama?" Baby Bear asked hopefully.

"No, of course not," was Mama Bear's quick reply. "You know how your father hates it when you play with your food."

"Aw, you never let me have any fun," Baby Bear said and skulked off to a corner of the room before returning a moment later with a knife and fork. "I'm hungry."

Papa Bear rubbed his paws together as he grinned wickedly, his canines flashing in the dim light of the shack. "We all are, kid. Well, let's get to it. It's time to eat."

The family of bears slowly went to the bed Goldie was sleeping in and surrounded it, each of the bears' mouth dripping with saliva in anticipation of the carnage to come.

Goldie was immobile, her eyes closed in death, her skin pale. The bears noticed none of this, only wanting to feed.

It was as Papa Bear pulled down the blanket Goldie had been under, exposing the body to all three hungry bears, that Goldie's eyes suddenly snapped open to look around her at the three bears before.

Now one of the living dead, Goldie felt no fear at the wild animals looking down on her, all she felt was a hunger rising within her.

But before she could act, Papa Bear was on her, and then so were Mama and Baby Bear.

Some time later after nightfall, the door to the small shack opened. Inside, the place was dark, shadows upon shadows filling the doorway.

Then a blood-soaked Goldie stepped outside. From head to toe she was covered in bear blood and in her hand was the front paw of Baby Bear. Her mouth had bits of fur stuck to it and she spit out a small piece of bone. Her stomach was distended now, full of bear meat, and she burped loudly as she took one last bite of the bear paw and tossed it away.

The bears were formidable creatures but then again, they had never tried to eat a zombie. Goldie's teeth and fingernails had been more than a match for the hungry bears, and in no time flat Goldie had killed Papa Bear, before then tearing apart Mama Bear while Baby Bear had watched in horror.

After Mama Bear had been killed, Goldie had taken her time with the little one, relishing the kill and the taste of young bear meat.

As Goldie walked off into the woods on her way back to the city so she could begin feeding on humans, she said, "The Papa Bear was much too tough, as he was old, and the Mama Bear had been too stringy, her muscles withered from lack of food, but Baby Bear had been just right, his meat tender and bloody. I can't wait to eat human meat, too. If it's half as good as bear meat, it'll be just perfect."

CINDER-ZOMBIE

MEAGAN JEFFREY

We all know the story of Cinderella, so you don't need to be filled in on all the small details of how Cinderella was beautiful, sweet, and lived with her evil, bitchy stepmother and even uglier and more evil stepsisters because her father had fallen ill and died.

I also don't have to tell you that her stepmother and stepsisters were very jealous of her beauty and worked her to the bone around the house, making her do all the cleaning, cooking, shopping, sewing, washing, laundry folding, etc.

I don't have to tell you any of that, but I just did.

But this story isn't about Cinderella, it's about someone else.

This is a story about Cindy Johnson.

Cindy kept her shoulder length, beautiful blond hair up in a bun all the time, never wore makeup, and dressed in ragged track pants and a sweater. She never bothered to dress nicely because she was never able to go out and see anyone or do anything because her evil stepmother and step sisters kept her very busy at home doing everything they were too lazy to do.

Cindy had a closet full of brand name clothes, beautiful dresses and fancy shoes and purses that she'd secretly been collecting, hoping that one day she would be able to wear them. Hoping that one day she would be rid of the evil bitches she lived with.

Cindy was out in the backyard of her house, raking the yard as her stepmother had told her to do, when she heard the crackling of leaves behind her on the other side of the fence. She turned to look and saw a man standing there looking at her, his face hidden in the shadow of the tree he stood beside. But she could see the outline of his face and saw that he was a handsome man. A brown fedora covered his hair, and he wore a blue t-shirt and loose faded blue jeans. He had a bit of scruff on his face.

He gave her a slight, sideways smile as she looked at him, making her turn away blushing. She knew she couldn't speak to him, shouldn't speak to him, because her stepmother and stepsisters would just shoo him away and then lock her up again in that tiny, smelly, dark room in the basement; with no light, food or water. That's how they liked to punish her.

So, Cindy turned away and continued to rake the leaves. When she looked back over her shoulder, she saw he was still there, but closer to the fence now.

"Hi," he said in a voice softer and sexier than she expected it to be.

Her heart stopped, her breath caught in her throat and she froze. She couldn't move or speak. She felt her face getting hot as her cheeks began to turn red. Then she gathered the courage to speak. She swallowed hard, breathed in deeply and let her breath out softly before saying, "Hello, yourself."

He smiled at her with a very kind smile. "What's someone like you doing out here cleaning the yard?" he asked. "Don't you have someone to do that for you?"

"No, I have to do it, or my stepmother will punish me," she answered meekly, lowering her eyes to the ground as the words came out.

The man looked shocked and upset upon hearing this. "Oh," he said quietly.

Cindy continued to rake near the fence so her stepmother wouldn't see her talking to the man.

"I'm Ford, nice to meet you. And you are?" he asked, sticking his hand out to shake hers.

She stopped raking, then took his cold hand in hers. "I'm Cindy, very nice to meet you, too," she said shyly.

She went to pull her hand from his but felt his grip tighten. She immediately became scared and started to panic. She tried to pull away but he wouldn't let go. "Let me go!" she said, frightened. But he was strong and wouldn't loosen his grip on her. He pulled her closer to the fence, pulling her arm hard up to his mouth. Then he bit her!

"Let me go! What are you doing?" she screamed. "Let me go!" She yelled over and over.

He let go of her arm and looked at her with glazed eyes. That's when he stepped out of the shadow of the tree and she realized that he wasn't as handsome up close as he was further back. That's when she noticed that his skin was so pale it was almost gray, and his teeth were yellow…he wasn't even alive!

"What the hell? What are you?" she asked, backing away from the fence while holding her arm as tears rolled down her face.

He let out a mean, evil laugh. "Why, I'm a zombie. Can't you tell? And now, you will be too and you can have your wish of not having to listen to your bitchy stepmother and stepsisters. You'll be able to get rid of them once and for all yourself. So, consider this a favor."

Cindy's eyes grew wide with fear; she started to cry harder and ran inside the house. She went straight to the bathroom to clean her wound. She washed it out in the sink, looking at the bite mark, wondering if he was just some psycho or if he was telling her the truth and she was now about to become the walking dead! She dried off her wound gently with a towel and put an antiseptic on it, then wrapped it in a bandage.

After making sure the man was gone, she went back out to the yard to finish her chores before her stepmother found out she wasn't working and punished her. Cindy looked around for Ford, wondering if he was lurking somewhere close, but she didn't see him. She finished raking the leaves, bagging them up and threw them away. As she headed back inside, she felt a twinge of pain in her stomach. She put a hand on the doorframe to hold herself up, wrapped her free arm around her waist and crouched over in pain. When the pain went away enough for her to walk, she went inside slowly.

She found her stepmother in the kitchen, standing there looking at her angrily. "What took you so long?" she demanded to know.

Cindy's eyes were wide with fear. "I…I'm sorry. I finished as fast as I could. I had to stop to clean a cut I got." She showed her stepmother the bandage on her arm.

"Next time bleed to death for all I care. When I say to get something done you get it done. I don't care if you get hurt. Do you understand me? Or would you like to go downstairs?" she snapped at Cindy.

"No, I wouldn't like to go down there. I'm really sorry. I'll do as you ask," she said meekly and lowered her eyes to the floor.

"Get out of my face; I can't stand to look at you. Go clean yourself up, you're filthy!" her stepmother ordered.

Cindy rushed away to the bathroom and ran a bath. She took her clothes off and noticed that her skin was turning gray like Ford's, and her eyes were turning yellow, as were her teeth. She unwrapped her wound and saw that it was worse than before and looked disgusting. It had green puss oozing out of it, rivulets of watery blood dripping and running out of it and it smelled like rotting, dead flesh. She knew then that he hadn't lied when she saw the state of her wound and felt terror upon knowing she was going to die; she started to panic. There was so much she still wanted to do with her life.

She climbed into the bathtub of hot water, and as she sat and soaked, she realized that even if she wasn't going to die, and though there were so many things she wanted to do with her life, she was never going to be able to do them because of her stepmother and stepsisters.

Then she remembered what Ford had said to her after he bit her and she smiled to herself. Soon, she would be free of those wicked bitches!

Cindy didn't know how long or painful it was to die or turn into a zombie and wasn't really looking forward to it. She was afraid that it was going to be really painful and a long process. Then came a banging at the bathroom door.

"Cindy, get your ass out here and make me some damn dinner!" her sister Anna yelled at her.

"Okay, one minute," Cindy called back. She quickly got out of the bath, got dressed, and just as she was about to open the door, she fell to the floor in pain. Her stomach was twisting and turning, her guts ached, and then she felt a stabbing pain in her chest and arm.

She couldn't catch her breath, her heart was pounding hard and fast, so much so that she thought it was going to explode inside her. Then her heart beats began slowing, her breathing became shallow and calmer. She fell on her side, clutching her stomach with both arms. She knew this was it, that she was dying. It wasn't nearly as bad as she expected it to be.

Cindy thought of how she wouldn't have to be a slave any more. As her heart came to a stop and her breathing ceased, Cindy's final thoughts were of her loving father whom she missed dearly.

Her sister Anna began banging on the bathroom door again, furious that Cindy wasn't listening to her. When she didn't answer, Anna opened the door and saw Cindy dead on the bathroom floor. She covered her mouth in shock, then gathered herself and bent down and closed Cindy's eyes. She ran downstairs to get her mother, not knowing what she should do with Cindy's body. She found her mother in the library and told her what happened. She, her mother and sister Dri went up to the bathroom and found Cindy lying there, lifeless.

"What do we do with her?" Dri asked her mother, confused.

"You can burn her out back for all I care," their mother said, furious. "Now what are we going to do for a maid?"

Dri and Anna looked at one another shocked at what she'd just said. They were mean to Cindy but they didn't actually hate her, they were just very jealous of her beauty and were terrified of their mother, so they acted like they hated Cindy. They actually felt very bad that she was dead.

"I'll bury her out back by the old Cedar tree," Anna said softly to her mother, looking at her for approval.

"Fine," her stepmother snapped and stormed away downstairs.

Anna looked at Dri, then peeked down the hall to be sure their mother was gone before saying to Dri, "I can't believe she died. What do you think happened? You don't think we worked her to death, do you?"

Dri looked sadly at Anna and then down at Cindy. "Maybe we did. It's not like mother let her sleep long at night or eat right. Maybe she had a heart attack or something. We have to get her out of here before Mother comes back and throws her in the fire pit out back."

The girls each picked up one end of Cindy gently and carried her out to the backyard over to the Cedar tree. Dri refused to dig the hole, so Anna reluctantly did it herself. After digging on and off for two hours, the hole was finished being dug deep enough that animals wouldn't smell her and dig her up. Anna jumped down in the hole and had Dri slowly and gently lower Cindy down to her. She softly laid the body down in the hole, crossed Cindy's arms over her chest and climbed out.

Dri threw down a beautiful baby blue blanket to cover the body, after helping Anna out of the hole. Then they started to throw the dirt back on top, burying Cindy.

When the grave was filled, they both went back in the house, told their mother it was done, and went upstairs to get cleaned up and go to bed.

The girls tossed and turned in their sleep that night. Their minds were restless with thoughts of Cindy dead on the bathroom floor and then burying her in the backyard like an animal. Their minds also raced of thoughts at how mean their mother really was and what was in store for them now.

Out in the backyard the fresh grave was moving and shaking. Cindy was digging her way out of her grave. She was digging hard and fast, determined to get out of the tight hole she'd been left to rot in. She still had the same memories she had when she was alive and the same feelings, she was just a lot more angry and hungry.

She found herself having a horrid craving for flesh, any kind of flesh. She didn't care if it was human, animal, dead or alive, she just really wanted to eat flesh!

She managed to get her hands and head out of the hole, looking around and shaking the dirt from her head, then she forced the rest of her body out of the hole. She brushed herself off and looked at the dark house. She was trying to decide if she wanted to go in yet and devour the girls and their bitch mother or wait.

That was when she heard a familiar voice behind her. "Hey there, you're finally dead are ya?" Ford asked her with a snicker.

Cindy turned around to look at Ford and saw a huge group of zombies with him. She couldn't believe her eyes and how many there were. There must have been over a hundred. She couldn't exactly tell or see them all.

"We're here to collect you," Ford said, staring her directly in the eye.

Cindy took a step back. "What do you mean collect me? Collect me for what?" she asked.

"To take over of course," he answered with a sneer.

Cindy looked at him, then at the others behind him, who were glaring at her. Some even hissed in anger at her.

"You'll have your chance with your family as promised," Ford went on to explain, "You'll have your chance at the Elements dance tomorrow night that they're going to. Your sisters are going to try and be chosen to marry Thomas Farrell, who is rich and has been searching high and low for the perfect bride."

"And we're going to just charge in?" Cindy asked confused.

"Of course not, that would create mass panic; we're going to send you in as one of them. You are 'Cindy' after all, and you're going to be the one he chooses. For when he does, you'll then be able to bite him. Then he will go home and start turning humans out West into zombies, and soon, everyone will be the walking dead."

Cindy's eyes widened in horror. She didn't like this plan much at all. She couldn't imagine the world being overrun with zombies. But in looking at the crowd behind Ford, she knew she had no choice but to agree.

At least for now.

Cindy climbed over the fence and went with Ford and the other zombies. They marched to downtown, stalking anyone and everyone who came into sight.

They were attacking anyone who they saw, biting them, tearing their flesh from their bodies, eating them alive. Screams were heard as far as one could hear, and people were running into buildings trying to hide, take cover and get away from them. But the zombies weren't like the ones in movies, these zombies were smart, fast and angry. They were just like humans only with exceptional speed and strength.

Cindy was standing in the middle of the street, watching the mass panic and horror. She didn't want to join in, but her stomach was twisting and turning again, giving her that twinge of pain. Her craving for flesh was taking over her every thought.

Just then a man ran in front of her, and she grabbed him. Pulling back the collar of his shirt, she threw him on his back to the road. With a thud and sound of air being knocked out of his chest, she straddled him, looking him in the eyes with one of the most evil looks he'd ever seen. He started to beg for his life, but it was pointless because she didn't hear him. Her craving was too strong; it had taken over her body and thoughts. She snarled, then bit him hard in the throat. Hot blood squirted in her face, hair and onto the ground. She kept biting him, tearing his flesh from his throat, exposing the muscles and tendons. She ate him alive, the man screaming in pain until he was dead and she couldn't eat another bite.

Ford was standing behind her, watching with pride in his eyes. "I knew you had it in you," he said, then ran after a woman who was trying to get away.

Cindy wiped her mouth clean with her arm and looked down at the man she had just eaten alive. She had no feelings of sadness or remorse, just a nothingness.

Bodies were strewn everywhere. Zombies were eating, some walking away and others taking the bodies to an alleyway to feed in private. Soon, all the bodies were taken to the alleyways.

"We always clean our mess," Ford told her. "That way when someone comes, they don't see the bodies and run or tell anyone. This way we have the advantage of the unknown." He finished and walked away.

"But what about all the blood on the ground?" she asked.

"That will fade away in time."

Cindy didn't know if she should follow him or not.

"Psst... Pssst..."

Cindy looked around and saw an elderly woman standing in the doorway of a store and wondered how the zombies had missed her. The old woman signaled to Cindy to come to her. Cindy looked around to see if anyone was watching, and when she was sure no one was, she quickly went into the building with the old woman, who closed the door behind her and locked it tight.

"My dear, you're such a lovely young woman, who's had much heartache and bad fortune." The old woman talked gently in an almost sing-song voice.

Cindy was surprised. "How do you know that? How do you know me?" she asked.

The old woman just smiled. "Just think of me as your Fairy Godmother," she said and then giggled.

Cindy looked at her puzzled, then laughed when she understood. "Fairy Godmother, right," Cindy said sarcastically.

The old woman smiled and sat down at a little coffee table, suggesting for Cindy to sit with her. "I can help you dear, I can make you human again, but you have to do exactly what I say. Do you want me to help you?" she asked in the same sing-song voice.

Cindy's eyes sparkled for a second with joy. "Yes, of course!"

"Okay, then this is what you have to do," the old woman said and quickly explained that Cindy would have to go to the dance, and make Thomas fall head over heals in love with her; then have him marry her within forty-eight hours.

The old woman would make Cindy look stunning, dress her in the most sexy, beautiful dress, shoes, accessories, and give her perfume that Thomas wouldn't be able to resist. She would make Cindy the Princess of the dance. But she could only keep the spell on Cindy until midnight, after that, Cindy was on her own for making him love her.

Cindy agreed, even though she didn't think it would work. The old woman also told her that when Thomas fell in love with her and they kissed, that the kiss would make them husband and wife, and that the curse of the zombies would be broken on all the zombies, not just her.

Cindy was excited to try; if it worked it would all be worth it.

The old woman kept Cindy hidden in the store until the dance the next night. She fed Cindy dead animals to keep her craving for flesh under control.

When it was time the old woman, who was obviously a witch, cast her spell on Cindy, making her the sexiest, most beautiful woman that would be at the dance. Cindy wore a gold mini-dress that had a U-shaped collar that went down to her belly button, showing a generous amount of skin; the back was backless.

She had matching gold sparkle high heels and a gold necklace. Her hair was perfectly straight and sleek. Her makeup was soft and gave her a sun-kissed glow. Her lips glistened and shined with the red lip gloss and she wore Armani Code perfume. The old woman promised that Thomas wouldn't be able to resist her or take his eyes off her. She would be the 'Belle of the ball.'

The old woman led Cindy outside to a pink limousine that was waiting for her. A chauffeur was standing at the car door, holding it open for her.

Cindy smiled at the old woman and gave her a hug and a kiss on the cheek. "This is a dream come true. Thank you." Then she got in the limousine and was whisked away to the dance.

When the limousine pulled up to the dance, Cindy saw a line almost a block long. She sighed, thinking of her time limit.

"Don't worry, Miss, you have a VIP pass, you get to walk right on in," the driver said, handing a VIP pass to her over his shoulder

Cindy took it and smiled. "Thank you," she said excitedly.

The driver parked the limousine right at the front doors of the dance and opened the car door for her. She saw that everyone in the line was watching the limousine, to see who was going to exit it. Cindy took a deep breath and eased out of the vehicle. Everyone was watching her. The women in the line gave her dirty locks of jealousy and the men smiled, winked and whistled at her. She handed her VIP pass to the doorman, and he lifted the red velvet rope for her and let her in.

Cindy walked sexily down the hall to where the dance floor was and the VIP room. Everyone had their eyes fixed on her as she passed them; she was the most beautiful and stunning woman there, just as the old woman had promised. The other women were angry; they knew if Thomas saw Cindy they didn't stand a chance.

Cindy stood at the side of the dance floor, looking at the dancers, gazing around to see where Thomas was. Then she saw her stepmother and sisters.

They saw her, too, but didn't know it was her. They'd never seen her dressed so beautifully and with makeup and her hair done.

Cindy smiled at them, walking right past them as she went to the center of the dance floor. She gave them a smug look as she glanced back over her shoulder.

"I know her from somewhere," Anna said to Dri.

Dri shrugged her shoulders unknowingly and just watched Cindy, who had made her way to the center of the dance floor and started dancing to the thumping music that was playing over the speakers.

People had made room for her. The other women dancing didn't want to be near her, for they were jealous of her beauty and the men just wanted to watch in awe as she danced.

She was out on the dance floor for no more than ten minutes when the spotlight was on her. She kept dancing, but turned to look up at the D.J. booth. Thomas was up there, pointing at her. The people around her were also looking up at the D.J. booth and also saw Thomas pointing down at her.

They instantly knew that he had chosen her.

Cindy smiled slyly and kept dancing. Thomas left the D.J. booth and walked down to her. Girls were touching his arms and back as he walked past them, trying to get his attention, even a glance from him, but his eyes were locked on Cindy.

The dancers made way for him when he started to walk towards Cindy. He gently tapped her on the bare shoulder; she turned and he was at a loss for words. She was stunning, the most beautiful woman he'd ever seen. He was instantly in love with her. She saw the love in his eyes and smiled. The D.J. lowered the music and put on a slow song.

Thomas took Cindy's hand. "Dance with me, please," he said.

She nodded and smiled.

As they danced, he caught the scent of her perfume, making his eyes flutter and heart race.

"It's nice to meet you, Thomas," she said, breaking the silence between them.

He smiled and replied, "Yes, it's very nice to meet you, too."

"My name's Cindy." She told him before he asked. Then she placed her head gently on his shoulder as they danced, knowing he could smell her perfume, feel her silky hair against his face and her bare skin on his hands. She softly kissed his neck, sending a wave of shivers down his spine. He took in a deep breath and as she lifted her head, he kissed her, passionately, eagerly and lovingly.

After their first kiss, he looked into her sparkling eyes and said, "You know that I'm here to pick a wife, right?"

Cindy smiled and nodded. "Yes, of course. That's why I came."

Thomas smiled even wider, happy that she was aware of this. "Would you like to be my wife? You're the most beautiful, most stunning woman I've ever seen. I would love to spend the rest of my life seeing your beauty every day and taking care of you, loving you. Will you marry me?"

A tear rolled down Cindy's cheek and she answered excitedly, "Yes! Yes, of course I'll marry you!"

Thomas smiled and gave her another kiss, holding her tight.

Cindy was relieved that her plan was going so well. Thomas took Cindy up to the D.J. booth and they announced that he had found his bride to be. The crowed cheered for them, although most of the women were angry.

When Thomas said that he'd found his bride and introduced her, Cindy's stepmother and stepsisters' mouths hit the floor. They couldn't believe what they had just heard. They had found her dead, and had buried her in the backyard. She couldn't be standing there and alive.

Cindy remembered she only had until midnight, then she would go back to looking like a zombie and she knew Thomas wouldn't want her anymore. She looked at the clock on the wall. It was 11:55 p.m. She panicked and gave Thomas a kiss. "I have to go. I'm sorry. I really have to go," she said and turned to leave.

"But how will I find of you again?" he asked, surprised at her sudden departure.

She quickly wrote down her phone number and gave it to him, "Call me in the morning, I'll explain then." Before he could say anything else, she rushed down the stairs, losing a shoe along her way down. She was in such a hurry she didn't stop to get it. Thomas saw the show and ran down to get it for her.

When he looked up, she was gone.

Cindy was already outside and running as fast as she could down the street, back to the store.

Then she saw Ford and the zombies standing there, looking at her.

Ford looked angry.

"So, you don't want to be one of us?" Ford growled at her angrily. "Well, that's okay, you can go, but we're not letting those humans at the dance go," he said, motioning for the other zombies to go to the dance.

She knew the zombies would kill everyone in there—including Thomas—and she panicked. "Please, please don't do this. Please don't kill him," she begged, sobbing

Ford stared at her, and for a split second he felt a twinge of human emotion: he cared. Then he snapped out of it and growled at her, "Tough."

He grabbed her by the arm and dragged her down the street back to an abandoned house, where he and some of the other zombies hid in the daytime.

As she entered the house, Cindy could hear people screaming and yelling, the voices mixed in with the growls and hisses of the zombies, even though she was blocks away. She knew people were being slaughtered. Then that craving came back to her, her sexy dress, hair, shoes, necklace and perfume all vanished and she was a zombie again.

Her craving was now even stronger than before, so strong she couldn't control it. She looked at Ford and snarled, then lunged at him. She bit him on the cheek, then neck, splattering blood all over her. Ford wasn't expecting her to attack him and wasn't ready to defend himself. By the time he realized what was going on, she had punched her hand through his chest and tore out his heart, holding it up in front of him as she ate it.

His eyes grew big in horror at the sight. Then she turned and looked around the house and spotted a large butcher knife on the kitchen counter. She dashed into the kitchen and picked up the knife, then ran back to Ford and cut his head clean off.

She held his severed head in her hand by the hair, looking at him. She felt bad that she had killed him so easily, but then felt a strong pain in her chest, stomach and body. It was just like the pain she'd felt when she'd turned into a zombie. She didn't understand why she was in pain again, then realized that no one was screaming anymore from outside. She crawled to the front door and looked down the road. She saw people running in terror, and saw zombies falling to the ground in pain—like her.

She saw the old woman standing in the middle of the street, smiling. The old woman walked down the street to where Cindy was and looked at her from the sidewalk. "I didn't tell you that you could also just kill him and break the curse," she told Cindy with a sly grin. "I left that to you to figure out." The old woman joined Cindy and stayed with her as she turned back into a beautiful human.

It took the rest of the night for Cindy and the other zombies to turn back to normal. Once Cindy was human again, the old woman told her that she would cast a spell so that no one would remember what had happened at the dance. They would only remember the dance and Thomas picking Cindy to marry.

She told Cindy that Thomas would be waiting for her at the church at twelve o'clock sharp, to marry her.

"But I don't have a wedding dress," Cindy said sadly.

"No, but you have me," the old woman said, then spoke a series of words Cindy didn't understand. The next thing Cindy knew, she was wearing her dream wedding dress. Her hair was in loose curls and her makeup just perfect, with that sun-kissed glow again and the same Armani Code perfume.

This time waiting to take Cindy to the church was a horse and carriage laced with pink flowers and lace.

Cindy arrived at the church where many people were standing outside, waiting to see her, to get a glimpse of her and take pictures.

She was helped out of the carriage and led into the chapel, where a well-dressed and handsome Thomas waited for her.

Out of the corner of her eye she saw Ford, standing there, looking at her sadly.

She walked over to him. "How are you here?" she asked him, shocked. He looked confused, then she remembered that the old woman had told her how no one would remember the zombies and figured that she'd made Ford alive and human again, like the zombies.

"I came because I had to tell you before it's too late that I love you," Ford said.

Cindy was happy and sad to hear this. Then she realized that the curse was already broken, she didn't have to marry Thomas, that she could be with Ford and marry him, her real Prince Charming.

She ran to Thomas who was waiting patiently and whispered in his ear that she couldn't marry him, that she loved Ford and wanted to marry him instead.

Thomas only nodded, as if he understood completely, and he quickly announced to the guests that there would be a delay and change in groom.

Everyone was confused as Thomas had Ford dress in his suit and sent him down to wait for his new bride. Thomas then introduced them as Cindy and her Prince Charming, Ford.

The priest married them, they kissed the deepest kiss of love, and were announced as husband and wife.

The zombie curse was over and Cindy was free.

She lived happily ever after.

RAPUNZEL OF THE DEAD

ANTHONY GIANGREGORIO

There were once a man and a woman who had long in vain wished for a child. But finally the woman believed that God was about to grant her desire as even now her belly grew large.

This young couple had a little window at the back of their house from which a splendid garden could be seen, which was full of the most beautiful flowers and herbs. It was, however, surrounded by a high wall, and no one dared to go into it because it belonged to an evil enchantress named Dame Gothel, who had great power and was dreaded by all the world.

One day the woman was standing by the window and looking down into the garden, when she saw planted the most beautiful rampion (a type of greens). It looked so fresh and green that she longed for it in a way that only a pregnant woman can do. She pined away constantly, and began to look pale and miserable.

Her husband was alarmed, and asked, "What ails you, my dear wife?"

"If I can't eat some of that rampion, which is in the garden behind our house, I shall simply die," she replied.

The man, who loved her, thought, *Sooner than let my wife die, I will bring her some of the rampion, and let it cost what it will.*

So at twilight, he clambered down over the wall and into the garden of the enchantress, hastily clutched a handful of rampion, and took it to his wife. She at once made herself a salad of it, and ate it greedily. It tasted so good to her—so very good—that the next day she longed for it three times as much as before. Unknown to her, the rampion had a spell on it that made the eater want it more and more until they could not contain themselves.

The husband knew that if he was to have any rest, he must once more descend into the garden. That evening, in the falling gloom, he scaled the wall again, but when he had clambered down the wall he was terribly afraid, for he saw the enchantress standing before him, her arms crossed before her, her face a mask of disproval.

"How dare you descend into my garden and steal my rampion like a thief," she said with an angry look. "You will suffer for your insolence!"

"Wait," he answered, "let mercy take the place of justice. I only made up my mind to do it out of necessity. My wife saw your rampion from the window, and felt such a longing for it that she would have died if she hadn't got some to eat. She is with child you see."

The enchantress allowed her anger to be softened, and said, "If the case be as you say, I will allow you to take away with you as much rampion as you will, only I make one condition, you must give me the child which your wife will bring into this world. It shall be well treated, and I will care for it like a mother. But if you deny me this I will withhold what you seek and she and the child will die of longing anyway."

The man in his terror consented to everything, and when his wife was brought to bed to give birth some months later, the enchantress appeared at once, gave the child the name of Rapunzel, and took it away with her, leaving the young couple to mourn their lost child.

Rapunzel grew into the most beautiful child under the sun. When she was twelve years old, the enchantress shut her into a tower, which lay in a forest. The tower had neither stairs nor a door, but at the top was a little window. When the enchantress wanted to go in, she placed herself beneath it and cried, "Rapunzel, Rapunzel, let down your hair to me."

Rapunzel had magnificent long hair, fine as spun gold, and when she heard the voice of the enchantress, she unfastened her braided tresses, wound them around one of the hooks of the window above, then the hair fell ten stories down. The enchantress climbed up it.

After a year or two, it came to pass that the king's son rode through the forest and passed by the tower. As he went by he heard a song, which was so charming that he stood still and listened. This was Rapunzel, who in her solitude passed her time in letting her sweet voice resound. The king's son wanted to climb up to her, and looked for the door of the tower, but none was to be found. He rode home, but the singing had so deeply touched his heart, that every day he went out into the forest and listened to it.

Once when he was standing behind a tree, he saw an enchantress arrive at the tower, and he heard how she called out, "Rapunzel, Rapunzel, let down your hair to me."

Then Rapunzel let down the braids of her hair, and the enchantress climbed up to her. "If that is the ladder by which one ascends to the tower above, then I too will try my fortune," he said, and the next day when it began to grow dark, he went to the tower and cried, "Rapunzel, Rapunzel, let down your hair to me."

Immediately the hair fell down and the king's son climbed up.

At first Rapunzel was terribly frightened when a man, such as her eyes had never yet beheld, came to her, but the king's son began to talk to her like a friend, and told her that his heart had been so stirred that it had let him have no rest, and that he'd been forced to see her.

Rapunzel lost her fear of him, and when he asked her if she would take him for her husband, and she saw that he was young and handsome, she thought, *He will love me more than old Dame Gothel does*, and she said yes, and laid her hand in his.

"I will willingly go away with you," she said, "but I don't know how to get down. Bring with you a skein of silk every time you come, and I will weave a ladder with it, and when that is ready I will descend, and you will take me away on your horse."

They agreed that until that time he should come to her every evening, for the old woman came by day.

The enchantress knew nothing of this, until once Rapunzel said to her in an absence of thought, "Tell me, Dame Gothel, how it happens that you are so much heavier for me to draw up than the young king's son, he is with me in a moment."

"Ah-ha! You wicked child," the enchantress cried. "What did I hear you say! I thought I had separated you from all the world, yet you have deceived me!" In her anger she clutched Rapunzel's beautiful tresses, wrapped them twice around her left hand, seized a pair of cutting shears with the right, and prepared to cut them off. "I shall cut off your tresses and then he can never climb up here to see you again." She was about to do just that when she paused, a sinister smile appearing on her lips. "But wait, I have an even better idea."

Rapunzel cringed in fear, knowing whatever the enchantress had in mind, it wouldn't be good.

The next evening the king's son arrived at the foot of the tower and cried, "Rapunzel, Rapunzel, let down your hair to me."

Immediately the hair fell down and the king's son ascended, but instead of seeing his dearest Rapunzel's beautiful and angelic face, he found a hungry zombie glaring back at him with white eyes and gaunt cheeks.

The enchantress had put a curse on Rapunzel, turning her into one of the walking dead. Now, all she longed for was her lover's flesh and she attacked as soon as the king's son climbed through the window.

The two grappled and fell onto the floor, where the king's son fought valiantly to keep the teeth of his beloved from tearing out his throat. Snarling like a wild animal, Rapunzel clawed at his face with her fingernails, her teeth clacking less than an inch from his nose.

The king's son used all his strength and shoved her off him, then he got to his feet.

Rapunzel fell to the floor and rolled across it, then got up as quick as a cat. She gazed at him with a wicked and venomous look, her mouth already open wide in anticipation of feeding. Then she charged him.

The king's son acted out of instinct, and though his heart would never have allowed him to do what he did next, the warrior sprit inside him was in control.

Reaching out to a small table by his side, he grasped the cutting shears the enchantress had left there and used them like a knife.

When Rapunzel came at him he stabbed her in the left eye, the tip of the shears piercing the eyeball as if it had been an over-cooked hen's egg.

The eye burst and squirted liquid outwards, some of it getting into his mouth, the king's son swallowed some of it, and tried to spit out the rest, gagging as he drove the shears deeper into his undead beloved's skull.

Rapunzel went slack in his arms and he laid his young love down, the guilt in what he'd done filling him to bursting. Consumed by so much guilt and sadness over the loss of his beloved, he turned and jumped out the tower window.

He landed on the hard-packed ground and was killed, but he didn't stay dead for long.

Unknown to the enchantress, the curse had contained a virus that could be passed on to more victims. The king's son had ingested Rapunzel's bodily fluids in the form of the squirting eye.

Within hours of his passing he slowly rose from the dead, his eyes now blank, his thoughts only of the hunger within him.

He staggered off to his kingdom to feed.

HANSEL AND GRETEL:
A ZOMBIE FABLE

ANTHONY ALEXANDER VALADE

Once upon there was a family with financial issues. This family lived outside of the main town near the large forest. They had moved from town recently because Teun—the father—owed money to some large and in charge people but didn't have enough to pay them off when it came time.

So he decided becoming a freelance lumberjack would be a good way to keep him untraceable, so he started cutting down trees in the forest to sell them for an easy profit.

One evening, after a very small-portioned meal at the dining room table, Wilda—his wife and the step-mother to his two children, sent Teun's two children to bed.

As they left the room she turned toward Teun and began to speak in a not so impressed tone. "Teun, what are we going to do? I love you so much, but according to our empty pockets and bank account we're poor and very close to the edge of destitution. The bills have added up to the point where we might lose this house and you haven't looked for a real job in years. How did you think moving out of town would work? All we have is our insurance plan left and we're starving—the children too."

"I told you, there was a call the other day with an order for logs. The man said he would pay a hefty amount for a truckload," Teun said.

"But, Teun, our clothes have holes all over them, and the children are starving, *we* are starving. This 'man' better be paying you enough; you can't just chop trees down in a forest you don't own."

"Calm down, Wilda, just wait until tomorrow. I promise everything will be all right."

As the couple went to bed that night the sun began to set. Slowly, the moon rose, bathing the land in darkness, the wind the only sound until the birds of morning awoke with the sun again.

Teun awoke at sunrise to get an early start on his workload; he'd spent hours alone grueling over the fact. By noon he was sweating buckets and decided to get a little help. "Hansel!" he called.

If there were a more swift animal, it didn't exist as Hansel ran around the corner to his father. "Yes, Father?"

"There's a very important man coming here later today to pick up some wood and I have to get it ready. Can you help?"

"Yes, Father, of course!"

"All right then. So this is what's going to happen: I'm going to chop a log in half, you remove the debris, set up another log and put the chopped parts in a neat little pile over with the rest of them by the tree. Okay?"

"Okay."

"Excellent, now set one up for me." Teun continued chopping logs until Wilda silently walked up behind him, embracing him with her arms around the chest.

"Teun," she whispered, "you shouldn't treat the children like slaves you know."

"Wilda, is that a joke?"

Gretel exited the house wearing a pink flowered apron along with yellow gloves. "Mother!" she yelled from the doorstep. "I finished cleaning the living room, do I do the bathroom or the kitchen next?"

Teun and Wilda laughed, sharing the moment. Wilda ignored Gretel, leaving her waiting at the doorstep.

"Are you almost done? You've been cutting logs since sunrise," Wilda said.

"Almost done, dear, just a little longer. Why? Did you want to go play hide and seek in the woods again?

They kissed.

"You'll just have to see and find out silly," she said. "What time is that man going to be here?"

"He said he would be here around three in the afternoon," Teun said. "It's about two now so he should be here shortly."

"Sounds good, then we can go get something to eat later."

They kissed again and Wilda returned to the house, brushing Gretel inside.

"All right Hansel, set up that wonky one over there," Teun said. "You're going to have to prop it for me to cut."

"What if you miss, Father?"

"I won't miss, I promise, and I never break a promise. Just make sure you hold it tight and straight."

"Okay." Hansel propped up the log, holding it tight, while shuddering with his eyes closed.

After lining up the axe with the center of the log, Teun raised it behind his head, about to strike. As the axe began to come down, Hansel's head drifted centimeters closer to the log.

Crack

"Hansel! Keep your face away from the log!"

Teun had misinterpreted his aim and Hansel's face was only a couple millimeters from the edge of the axe.

Hansel fell back with tears in his eyes.

"Don't cry, son, there's no reason to. Nothing bad has happened to you."

Inside the house Gretel was talking to her step-mother. "Mother, what's for supper? My stomach is making noises."

"I'm not too sure, your father hasn't been paid yet so we're all just going to eat the stale bread in the cupboard," Wilda replied.

"I hope we don't."

As they sat in the kitchen relaxing, a pair of headlights caught their attention from outside through the window.

"Oh, there's the man who supposed to pay him," Wilda said.

Outside, Teun leered at the vehicle with tinted windows. Waiting for the occupant to exit the truck, he slammed his axe into the chopping log. The truck turned off and it was silent until the man stepped out.

"Hello, how are you today?" Teun said.

"I'm fine. I'm guessing you're Teun. I spoke to you on the phone the other day."

"Yes, that would be me. Are you alone or planning on putting the wood in the truck yourself? That's a lot of wood to move."

"Well, how about I pay you an extra hundred dollars if you move it for me."

"Two-hundred and we have a deal," Teun said,

"I don't care; I'll give you two-fifty. Just get it on the truck. I have other things to do today." The man lit a cigarette and exhaled forcefully while Teun began to load the wood onto the truck. Hansel tried to help his father by passing him a few pieces, but with him being so small it was cute.

Eventually all the wood was transferred onto the truck Teun dismounted as he wiped his hands on his pants and then went over for a handshake with the man.

The man grabbed Teun's hand and pulled him right up close, holding a small pistol to Teun's chest discreetly. "Obviously, you can see what's going on here. How do you want this to work out? Shall I leave you here dead in a pool of blood for your child to see, or are you just going to cooperate and let me leave?"

With a stone cold look on his face Teun said, "You can leave, but…" Teun pulled the man's face closer. "If I ever see you again, unarmed…"

"Let's just say you better not." The man smiled. "Well, I guess that's a threat if I've ever heard one." He pushed Teun away from him, then wiped himself off. "Pleasure doing business with you, pal." He tipped his hat at Teun as he entered his truck and drove off.

Teun picked up a large stone from the ground and threw it aggressively at the truck but missed. He muttered expletives under his breath. "Come on Hansel, let's go inside."

"Does that mean we get to eat now? I'm starving."

"We'll have to see, okay?"

"Okay."

Teun and Hansel walked into the house to greet Wilda, who had changed her clothing to be ready to go out and buy food. Meanwhile, Gretel was pretending to stir and taste invisible food in the pot on the ground in front of her.

"How much did he give you, Teun?" Wilda asked.

"I think we should talk."

"What do you mean, Teun?"

"Let's go talk in the other room," he said.

"All right children come and sit at the table; your father and I are just going into the other room to talk. We'll be right back."

The children sat at the table getting ready to eat while Teun and Wilda walked into their bedroom.

Wilda had entered the room with her arms crossed ready to listen to what Teun had to say. As Teun followed her inside, he locked the door behind them.

"I'm afraid your are going to be very upset with me in a couple seconds," he said.

"Why would that be, Teun? What happened?"

"Because the man that was here earlier held me at gunpoint and said that if I didn't let him leave without paying he was going to kill me."

Wilda's face turned sour as she stared at her husband. "Does that mean we have no food?"

"Yes, dear..."

"So our children have to eat stale bread and I have to wear these rags until you make some money?"

"Yes, dear...."

Wilda stormed out of the room. They saw their mother's face was filled with sadness. She prepared the loaf of stale bread and put it on the table. "Here you go, little ones. This is the best we can do." She stormed back into the bedroom, leaving Hansel and Gretel at the table by themselves.

"Hansel, are we poor?" Gretel asked.

"I think we are, I didn't see the man pay father."

"This bread is hard. I want something better. I miss Halloween, it's the best 'cause we get to go out and get free candy and that tastes way better."

Hansel grabbed a piece of bread and attempted to chew on it, but it was stale and he couldn't stomach swallowing it.

As he regurgitated it, Gretel's jaw dropped and she plugged her nose.

"Gross, Hansel! I'm telling Mother!"

"I think she's busy right now, can't you hear her arguing with Father?"

"I guess they are."

Mother gets mad at him a lot."

"Yes I know, but it's probably just an adult thing. The man outside must have been angry too 'cause he pushed father."

Both children's stomachs began to rumble.

"I'm hungry..."

"I know, Gretel, maybe there will be something to eat tomorrow."

Gretel answered Hansel through her yawning. "I hope so Hansel."

"Well, I think I should take you to bed now. It's getting late."

Gretel yawned again, nodding her head in agreement.

As Hansel left the table, he grabbed some pieces of bread and stuffed them in the waistband of his pants to hide and eat later.

He knew when he was hungry enough, even the bread would taste good.

Grabbing his younger sister's hand, he guided her to their bedroom and tucked her into bed before following.

"Goodnight, Gretel."

"Sweet dreams, Hansel."

As the two children lay down to sleep that night a light thunderstorm culminated outside. The house had become silent.

Until midnight.

Teun had stormed into the children's room with their jackets. "Hansel, get up and get dressed and put your jacket on."

Both children awoke in a daze.

"What's going on, Father?" Gretel asked, yawning.

"Don't worry about it, Gretel, just get your jacket on," Teun said.

Wilda entered the bedroom with tears in her eyes. "Here now, Gretel, put your jacket on like your father says."

"What's going on, Mother?"

"All of us are going for a nice stroll through the forest, okay? Now be a good little girl and let me help you put your jacket on," Wilda said.

Teun and Wilda helped their children with each child's respective jacket and shoes. Then the family headed for the front door.

Teun had been pulling Hansel by his arm and the boy accidentally brushed his face against the edge of a corner, producing a small cut that began to bleed profusely.

"Ouch, Father!"

"Sorry, Hansel. Here, take these tissues; hold one over your cut so you don't get blood everywhere." Teun handed Hansel a small package of tissues. Hansel immediately opened them up and held one to his face.

"Are you ready to do this, Teun?" Wilda asked.

"There's no time like the present, Wilda."

"Hansel, hold on to your father's hand, and Gretel, you hold on to mine, sweetie," Wilda said.

The family left the house and began to walk through the forest. The wind was subtle that night and with the thunderstorm overhead the lighting flashes were creating shadowed objects in the children's eyes.

"Mother, it's scary in here."

"Just be quiet, Gretel."

There was a crack overhead and Gretel screamed.

"It's just the lightning, Gretel. Everything will be okay, I promise, and what doesn't Father do?"

"Father doesn't break promises?" she said.

"That's right, sweetie, Father doesn't break promises."

"How is that cut doing, Hansel?" Teun asked.

"It's doing okay, Father, but it's still bleeding."

"If the tissue gets covered in blood just throw it away and use a new one," he said.

Hansel dropped the tissue onto the path but while reaching for another one he tripped on a tree root, falling onto his stomach. He landed hard crushing most of the stale bread that was still in his pants pocket. His father lifted him back up to his feet by the arm and they continued to walk.

As they walked down the path, bread crumbs gradually fell out and down to the ground from Hansel's pants.

The forest seemed to go on forever. The family walked until they were far from home. The trees seemed to get taller and larger the farther they walked, until it got to the point where the trees were blocking out the thunderstorm, sky, and any light possible.

Then they stopped.

"Wilda, I think this will be sufficient enough."

"Okay, Teun."

Wilda looked down at the children, almost crying but holding it back. "Do you guys want to play hide-and-go-seek?"

The children stayed silent.

"It'll be okay, I promise. Come on, you're a big boy. Aren't you, Hansel?" Teun asked.

"Yes, Father, it's just dark and I can't see anything."

"Well, both of you close your eyes and count to one hundred and then come looking for us, okay?"

"Okay."

"Okay."

They began counting and as the children began to count, Teun and Wilda ran away hand in hand, abandoning their children to be lost in the woods.

The children stood alone, counting, unaware of what their parents had done to them. Suddenly the silent air was filled with a dry cackle. The counting stopped immediately and their eyes opened when Hansel and Gretel heard it, causing Gretel to whimper in fear.

"Hansel, I'm scared."

"Me too, Gretel, but it'll be fine, we just have to finish counting."

"But where did Mother and Father go?"

"We have to find them, we're playing hide-and-go-seek remember?"

"I'm cold, Hansel."

He grabbed his sister by the hand and guided her to one of the largest trees near them, making them look very insignificant beside the massive trunk.

Again, the cackle echoed through the forest, and this time both children started to cry.

That night, the sound of crying shrouded the silence of the forest until Hansel and Gretel fell asleep, both too scared to move.

The next morning Gretel awoke shaking and starving. "Hansel, wake up! We have to find Mother and Father."

Hansel snapped awake, surprised by still being in the forest. "I'm not sure where we are, Gretel. Every direction looks the same."

"I'm hungry, Hansel."

"I know, I am too. Here I took some bread last night from the table." He reached into his pants to retrieve the bread but unfortunately only found crumbs. "Oh no. I think I dropped them in the forest."

"Oh, Hansel. What are we going to do?"

Hansel scanned the forest, looking for a way out. "I think we came from that way." He stood up, taking Gretel's hand and began to guide her through the forest.

As they walked Gretel was watching her footing. "Hansel, are those breadcrumbs?"

"I think they are. Hey, look at that, there's a path of them! If we follow it we should get back home!"

"Good, because I'm so hungry."

The two children followed the path of breadcrumbs. As they walked, the forest seemed to go on forever but neither child noticed how the trees were not getting any smaller but quite the opposite.

After walking for hours, Gretel fell down to the ground, exhausted.

Hansel tried to console her. "Gretel, are you okay? It's just a little bit farther. I think I can see the path."

Gretel didn't respond, so Hansel lifted her up into his arms and carried her. He was right though, there was a path ahead riddled with breadcrumbs.

Afraid of what was wrong with his sister, Hansel began to run down the path. When the end of the path was in his sights, he picked up speed. It seemed that the sun was setting extremely fast, and the closer he was to the end of the path the darker it became.

59

"Look, Gretel! We're almost home!"

Gretel was still unconscious and didn't respond.

Hansel came to the end of the path at what seemed to be sunset; he seemed very confused looking around the clearing. "That's not our house."

He stared at the house before him riddled with confusion. He looked behind him at the trail of crumbs and spotted a small shape in the far distance slowly working its way toward him and Gretel.

He stood silently, waiting to see what the shape could be and to his surprise it was a small, gold-colored creature eating the breadcrumbs.

An armadillo walked right up to Hansel and licked the rest of the crumbs off the boy's pants before it ventured back into the trees.

Hansel had never seen an animal like that before and had no idea what it could have been, but that wasn't the problem right now; he was more concerned about his sister.

He looked back to the house and then at the path, but the path was now gone and all that was there were dense woods. He quickly turned back around and found that the house was now dressed up like a Gingerbread house.

Eager to help his sister, he ran up to the house for help. Just as he entered the yard, the sun had finished setting and the only light was illuminated from the windows of the house.

Hansel slowly walked to the strange house and knocked on the front door.

"Who is it?" a female voice came from behind the door.

"Hansel and Gretel, ma'am. We're lost in the forest. My sister fell asleep while we were walking down the path and she won't wake up, please help us."

The door slowly opened and in the doorway stood a beautiful woman with long black hair wearing a frilly black dress. "Oh my.

You two are very young; how did you manage to end up in the forest all by yourselves?"

"Our mother and father brought us into the forest last night to play hide and seek with them." Hansel explained. "They told us to count to one hundred and then they were gone. We're so hungry and haven't eaten, please help us."

"Well, we can't have that. How about you two come in and make yourselves at home."

"Thank you, ma'am." Hansel carried Gretel into the house and removed his shoes.

"Just go put your sister on one of those two small beds near the fire. I'll fix you up something to eat," the woman said.

"Thank you, ma'am."

"That makes me feel kind of old, just call me Aunty, all right?"

"You're my mother's sister?"

"Sure, and I think I'll call to tell her you two have ended up here."

"Thank you, Aunty," he said.

The woman giggled at what Hansel said while walking into the other room. Hansel carried his sister to one of the beds and placed her down to remove her shoes and jacket.

"Are you all right, Gretel?"

Gretel stayed silent.

As Hansel turned around, he noticed how nice of a place the woman had. It was more of a cabin on the inside but everything looked very new and clean. His stomach rumbled from the sweet aroma of baked goods and candy that was scattered about on the counters and tables.

"Here you go, Hansel." The woman entered the room with a tray full of decorated gingerbread cookies of boys and girls.

"Whoa! I haven't had a cookie in forever! They smell delicious and they kind of look like Gretel and me," he said happily.

"Well, let's just hope they taste as good as they look then." As the woman placed the tray of gingerbread cookies onto the table, Hansel abruptly snatched one, burning his hand. The cookie fell to the floor, breaking apart.

"Ouch! I'm sorry I shouldn't have grabbed it like that. I've just been hungry for so long," he said.

"Is your hand all right, Hansel?"

"Yes, it doesn't hurt that bad now."

"Let me get you some milk, if you keep the glass in your hand, the burning sensation should be numbed by the time you finish it. Just make sure to drink it slowly."

While Hansel concentrated on waving his hand about, the woman walked into the kitchen and prepared a glass of milk for him.

"Just keep this in your hand until you finish it and your hand will feel better in no time."

"Thank you, Aunty."

"You're welcome, Hansel. Come and sit down near the fire and I'll get you some cookies that aren't piping hot."

Hansel took a large drink of his glass of milk while he walked over and sat down in front of the fireplace. The woman opened a cupboard in the kitchen and took out a large gingerbread boy decorated exactly like Hansel. She then approached Hansel.

"How is your hand doing, Hansel?"

"The glass feels cold."

"Excellent, just keep it on your hand."

The woman approached Hansel, presenting him with the gingerbread boy cookie. As Hansel snatched it out of her hand, a stern look came over her face.

"Didn't your parents ever teach you any manners?" she asked, irritated.

"Sometimes."

"Apparently you've been taught to starve as well I see. You're far too skinny, little Hansel, your sister too."

Hansel nodded in agreement while devouring his gingerbread boy, then he finished the rest of his milk immediately following the last bite.

"Can I have some more milk, Aunty?"

The woman rudely snatched the glass out of Hansel's hand and stiffly walked back to the refrigerator.

"Aunty, my stomach doesn't feel so good," he said.

The woman smirked as she replied, "Well, I guess you better go lay down in the other bed. It's late and you two should have been asleep hours ago."

Hansel slowly came to his feet in a daze. His vision began to blur as he shambled towards the small bed. Two steps away from the bed, his vision became dark and he fell into a paralyzing deep sleep, landing with his head striking the bed-frame before he fell onto the floor.

Several hours later, Gretel awoke in a panic, finding herself alone in a strange place she had never been before. The smell of baked goods and candy aroused her senses, and in an almost trance-like state, she slid off the bed and dashed towards the refrigerator.

As Gretel opened the fridge door, she peered inside, finding it to be completely empty except for one large pitcher of milk. She grabbed the large pitcher with both hands and brought it to her mouth, but before she could drink a single drop a door slammed closed behind her. Startled, she dropped the pitcher onto the floor, staying completely still as the pitcher broke and shattered around her feet, sending milk spraying in all directions.

"Hello, Gretel, I see you're finally awake," the woman said with a smile.

"Who are you? Where's my mother?" Gretel demanded.

"Listen, dear, you passed out in the woods. Your brother brought you here."

"I see you've made yourself at home already, Gretel."

"Where's Hansel?"

"He's waiting in the basement for you to wake up. Would you like to see him?"

"Yes, take me to Hansel."

"Just follow me." The woman approached Gretel, putting her hand on the back of her head and began to guide the girl to the basement.

Gretel stopped at the door, her eyes shrinking and body shaking. "Miss, may I have a cookie?"

The woman frowned at the question. She stepped back and slammed the door closed, only missing Gretel's face by centimeters. "Wait here, Gretel." She walked over to the kitchen and opened a cupboard, then grabbed a gingerbread girl and tossed it at Gretel. As Gretel looked down at the cookie on the floor before her, she noticed the resemblance between herself and the cookie and thought it was uncanny.

"Excuse me, Miss, do you happen to know me? This cookie looks just like me."

"I'm your Aunty child; do you want the cookie or not?"

"It's broken on the floor."

"Just pick it up and eat it. I thought you wanted to see your bother."

Gretel scooped up the pieces of cookie and began to gnaw them to bits as the woman walked back over and opened the basement door.

"Come on, Gretel, you go first. Don't worry how dark it is; there's light at the end."

Gretel slowly walked down the stairs, cautiously reaching to feel each step. The woman followed her down with an annoyance in her disposition.

"You're taking forever, Gretel. Just get to the bottom already!"

Gretel reached the last step, looking around for the light switch. In front of her was a closed door outlined in a white light. She entered the door with the woman following right behind her.

Gretel found herself in a large basement. The walls were empty except a large sheet covering a large part near the corner, the entire room made of gray concrete. There was an enormous metal oven with a handle, off to the side and attached to the furnace.

As the woman entered the room, she closed the door behind her while locking it secretly with a key on a necklace.

"You said Hansel was going to be in here! Where is he?"

"He's dead, child."

"What do you mean he's dead?" Gretel asked.

"I said dead, just like you're going to be."

While the woman chased Gretel around, the terrified little girl let out a bloodcurdling scream that she held until finally running out of breath.

While running around the basement, Gretel grabbed the large sheet, causing it to fall down. Both woman and child stood still as to what was hidden behind the sheet was exposed to Gretel.

The large sheet had covered a large cage made of metal Inside the cage was Hansel.

"Hansel!" Gretel yelled.

"He can't hear you, dear."

"Let him out! Now!"

The woman lunged forward and grabbed Gretel by her arm, then she held her up so they could interact face to face.

"Now, be a good little girl and be silent."

"Hanseeeellll!"

Looking down the woman's chest, Gretel spotted the key necklace. Quickly trying to come up with a plan, she ended up spitting in the woman's face.

In a fit of rage the woman threw Gretel to the floor and walked toward the door to go upstairs.

"You're going to pay for that, little girl!"

As the woman left, she slammed the door behind her and locked Gretel inside the basement.

Gretel ran up to the door, but after noticing she couldn't open it, she ran back to Hansel. "Wake up, Hansel!"

"You don't have to yell, Gretel, I'm awake." Hansel shook his head and climbed into a kneeling position.

"Hansel! You're not dead!"

"No, I'm not, but you have to stop yelling and listen to me, okay?"

Gretel nodded in agreement, giving Hansel her full attention.

"That lady is not our Aunty, okay? She's a witch. She gave me some milk and cookies and I fell asleep and woke up in here. Do not eat or drink anything she gives you. What you need to do is get out of this house and run back home to get help."

"I can't do that by myself, Hansel, the forest scares me!"

"It's okay; you're a big girl. You have to, or else both of us will never see Mother and Father again! Understand?"

"Yes, Hansel."

"Good, now I'm going to pretend I'm still sleeping so she will leave me alone. Just keep screaming my name until she comes back. Be careful."

"I will, Hansel."

Hansel laid back down on his back as Gretel began to scream, "Hansel! Wake up, Hansel! Hansel!"

Gretel ran over to the locked door and started to punch and kick it as hard as she could.

Then a bang came from the other side of the door. It was so loud it startled Gretel and caused her to fall back.

Slowly, the door was opened by the witch; she was holding a claw device that would fit around a child's neck. When she saw it, Gretel screamed even louder.

Taking what courage she could from her brother and knowing she had to be brave, despite being petrified, Gretel scrambled to her feet and ran straight at the witch. Quickly, the witch reacted by trying to grab her but was kicked in the shin instead. With the witch standing on one foot and in pain, Gretel pushed her over and tried to snatch the key necklace.

But with the necklace almost in reach, the witch grabbed Gretel's foot, but then received a swift kick in the nose instead. Ripping with all her might, Gretel pulled the key necklace off the witch's neck and ran up the stairs. In a panic, she ran out of the house without putting her shoes on.

Regaining herself, the witch stood back up with blood pouring down her face. "That little brat is going to pay for that!" As the witch approached the large furnace, she held her arms out and began to chant in a strange language. As she spoke, her skin aged and became discolored.

A large fire erupted inside the oven beside the furnace as she chanted. The door of the oven flew open, throwing large metal racks with burnt-to-a crisp cookies. As the racks and cookies collided with the opposing wall, the fire roared and became much larger to the point where the flames seemed to be reaching out from the giant oven as the witch continued chanting.

"You will rise! You will live once again! Listen, as I am the one who has summoned you! Thou shall do my bidding!"

A loud scream echoed in the basement, accompanied by a giant face of fire from the oven. Then, in an instant, the oven door slammed closed and the fire extinguished itself, leaving only smoke to clear up in the room.

"Rise!"

The oven door suddenly slammed back open, releasing all the smoke trapped inside, revealing the witch's creation in front of her.

"Hear my voice and know that your life belongs to me. Rise!"

As the words left her mouth, the creature's eyes burst open with an intense color of red. Slowly, the creature emerged from the oven, presenting itself in front of its master.

The creature overshadowed the witch with a height of six feet tall. Its skin constantly rotted and fell off like a slimy paste. Insides and intestines sealed the pronounced look, as they could be seen through holes in the skin. Its face was of a demented teenager with a crazed look that had lost most of its scalp, including hair.

The witch now appeared as an old woman, after using most of her life force to bring the creature into reality. "There's a child in the forest. Fetch her," she commanded. She raised an arm, her index finger pointing towards the stairs, and with a burst of energy the creature complied by rushing up the steps.

The witch then turned her attention to the cage. "Wake up, Hansel."

The boy didn't move.

"Stop pretending to sleep. I know the spell has worn off."

Hansel brought himself to a kneeling position.

"So, Hansel, are you still hungry?"

Gretel had been running through the forest at such a fast pace that she tripped over an errant tree root sticking out of the ground. She fell on her arm the wrong way, twisting her wrist. Lying on the ground in pain, she began screaming and crying, her sobs echoing though the forest. "Father!" she cried.

From somewhere nearby a foot stepped on a branch, the snap filling the air.

"Who is that? Who's there?"

More branches breaking suffused the air.

"Hello? Father? Mother? My arm hurts! Please make the pain go away!"

Several more branches snapped and echoed from every direction.

"Help me!" she called out.

From behind the tree that Gretel was lying in front of strolled out a small animal. Startled and weary, the armadillo slowly approached the crying Gretel with a slight whimper.

"Aww, aren't you the cutest thing! What's that around your leg?" Gretel asked, her arm forgotten.

The armadillo had thick string wrapped around its leg so tight that it was cutting off blood circulation to its foot and causing its leg to bleed.

Gretel stopped crying immediately, sat up, and motioned to the small animal as it came closer to her. As she picked it up with her good arm, the armadillo squirmed around.

She placed the armadillo back on the ground and began to pet it like a cat, telling it everything was going to be okay as she leaned down and began to pull off the string.

After removing the string, the armadillo's wound completely vanished and on further inspection she noticed a bloody used tissue caught between one of the other legs and removed it.

"This must be Hansel's! The one he used and tossed away when he cut himself. Do you know the way home, little guy?"

The armadillo didn't speak English and decided to curl up next to Gretel instead. She smiled and began to pet it as she locked around her surroundings.

"How am I ever going to find my way home through this forest?"

More tree branches could be heard breaking in the distance.

"Oh no, what's that?"

The armadillo seemed very alarmed at the sound and ran behind the tree. Gretel put the bloody tissue in her pocket with the key and followed the armadillo.

Loud screams echoed all around them as they waited to see who or what was coming their way.

Suddenly, the witch's creature appeared. When it reached the tree Gretel had been leaning against, it suddenly stopped to sniff the air awkwardly.

The creature twitched as it slowly smelled its surroundings. Quickly it turned to the neighboring tree where Gretel had left the armadillos string and bent down to sniff the blood. Hissing at the odor, it shot back up and walked toward the tree that was hiding Gretel and the armadillo.

As the creature approached the tree, Gretel could hear it coming closer and held back her tears while the creature sniffed the opposite side of the tree.

Suddenly, a large spider dropped down from a high branch on its line and onto Gretel's shoulder, causing her to scream and call attention to herself.

The creature screamed and moved around the tree and found Gretel. Staring her down with its fire red eyes, it began to drool and hiss at her. With one leap, it grabbed her and threw her to the ground, causing her to fall on her hurt arm. The spider landed on the ground and scurried away into the underbrush.

When the creature had thrown her down, Hansel's bloody tissue fell out of her pocket. The creature gave no attention to Gretel, but instead dropped to the ground and sniffed the bloody tissue.

After letting out a low moan, it got back to its feet and ran off in the other direction.

The armadillo grabbed the bloody tissue in its mouth and began to chase after the creature. With no time to think, Gretel followed them.

"How hard is it to find a little girl in the woods? I might as well have gone and caught her myself!" The witch was waiting at her dining room table with a plate of gingerbread cookies in the shape of boys, shaking her head in anger. "Well, I guess let's see how Hansel is doing."

After picking up the tray of cookies, the witch slowly made her way down the basement stairs. When she reached the last step, her creature burst through the front door, breaking it into pieces and then barreling down the stairs, knocking the witch to the floor.

The armadillo and Gretel were not too far behind the creature. They had just made it to the clearing where the house stood, and were making their way up to the door, where they could hear the witch yelling from downstairs. "What are you doing? That's not the little girl!"

The armadillo brushed up against Gretel, trying to get her attention. Gretel looked down as the armadillo presented her with the bloody tissue. Nodding in agreement, she grabbed the tissue and headed into the house and down the stairs.

The creature was banging on the cage, trying to get Hansel.

"That's enough, you delinquent! That's not the girl!" the witch yelled.

"Am I the girl?"

The witch spun around in haste at the sound of Gretel's voice. "There she is! Get her!"

The creature turned around and darted toward Gretel. As soon as it was close enough, Gretel raised the bloody tissue, causing the creature to stop and smell it. Once again it turned around and began to go after Hansel.

"Hansel!" Gretel ran up to the cage as well to find that Hansel had grown quite large in weight and was taking up a third of the cell.

"Hansel? Why are you so fat?"

"It was the witch!"

Completely frustrated, the witch yelled out at Gretel, "BECAUSE I'M GOING TO EAT HIM, AND YOU TOO!"

The witch began to chant towards the furnace again, causing a large fire to erupt in the oven.

"HEAR ME, ZOMBIE! FEAST UPON THE LITTLE GIRL OR ELSE YOUR BODY WILL FOREVER BE TOURTUED IN THE DEPTHS OF HELL!"

While the witch continued chanting, Gretel quickly moved up behind her and placed the tissue in the witch's dress pocket, then ran to the far wall.

"Come before me beast and recognize your creator!" she chanted in the strange language.

In a trance-like state, the creature presented itself before the witch, kneeling on one leg.

"Your damned soul is mine to control! I shall feast on these children like I feasted on your mother, father and brothers!"

The creature's face became enraged and its eyes began to glow red. It looked at Hansel and Gretel, then back towards the witch.

The witch finished chanting as the creature stood up straight and said, "It's people like you that give the title of Witch a bad name."

"Excuse me?" she asked, shocked that her minion had spoken.

The creature walked up to the witch and grabbed her by the hair, then said softly into her ear, "Murderer."

The creature then dragged her into the roaring fire projecting out of the oven. The witch's screams filled the room. When they were completely inside, the door of the oven slammed shut, leaving only smoke and the smell of burnt cookies in the air.

Gretel ran to Hansel almost in tears. "Hansel! Hansel! Are you all right?"

"My stomach hurts, no more cookies, please," he replied.

"How are we going to get you out of there?"

The armadillo descended to the bottom of the steps and dropped a gold key. Gretel smiled as she ran up to get the key. "Thank you, little guy!"

She ran back to the holding cell with the armadillo following her to unlock the cage door.

With all her might, she attempted to turn the key in the lock but it wouldn't budge. The armadillo whimpered at her and rubbed up against Gretel to get her attention while shaking its tail.

Gretel picked up the armadillo and pointed its tail near the key, and as she did this, the armadillo with almost no effort unlocked the cage. Before Gretel could put it back down, the armadillo reached over and began to lick her wounded arm.

As Gretel laughed from its tongue tickling her skin, she accidentally dropped the armadillo. The animal rolled through the bars of the cage and curled up beside Hansel, who looked down at the creature that had ate his breadcrumbs; he picked it up and held it in his hands.

The armadillo began to glow, the light became so blinding that neither child could look at what was happening. When the light faded, both children were perfectly healthy, clean, and back to their proportioned size, and they were now upstairs, sitting before the fireplace.

"What just happened, Hansel?"

"I'm not too sure, Gretel."

There was a knock on the door.

"Should we answer it?" she asked.

Hansel and Gretel both scrambled to their feet and raced to the door. Hansel grabbed the handle and pulled open the door.

"Hansel and Gretel, we found you" Teun said, relieved to have found his children.

Both children screamed in excitement and pounced on their father.

"Father! Me and Hansel met a witch!" Gretel said happily.

"Oh? And where is she?" Teun asked.

"She was pushed into a fire by a dead person!"

"Who lives here?" he asked.

Both children looked at each other in confusion, contemplating the question.

Gretel whispered into Hansel's ear and his eyes lit up. "Can we live here, Father?" he asked Teun.

"We can't just live here, Hansel, someone else has to be living here. Let's get a good look inside," Teun said.

Hansel and Gretel led their father inside the home.

"Wow, it looks a lot smaller from the outside. Hey, look, there's even another level!" Teun walked over to the staircase that was no longer going down, but up. He reached the attic door but to his surprise the door was locked. "Hey! Do either of you see a key anywhere down there?"

The children looked around the main floor but couldn't find anything until Gretel felt the outside of her pocket. She reached into her pocket and her eyes lit up as she removed a silver key. Gretel ran up the stairs and gave it to Teun, who then unlocked the door. A bright light blinded them for a second, but as their eyes focused, they found the attic to be full of ancient treasures made from gold and silver.

Each of their jaws dropped one by one, astonished by what they had found.

"So, whoever lived here died in a fire right?" Teun asked.

"Yep, we both saw it!" Gretel said.

"Excellent."

"Father?"

"Yes, Gretel?"

"Where's Mother?"

"Umm...I made her leave me so I could cash in on the insurance plan."

"Father?"

"Yes, Hansel?"

"There's blood all over the bottom of your pants and shoes."

"No more questions, kids."

PRINCE DREAMSHINE AND THE WALKING DEAD

SHANE KOCH

In a flash of rainbow sparkles, Fufflemuff, the gossamer-winged pink unicorn, flew through the air. Over the rustling green canopy of Furthest Forest, The Last Place, the mighty animal swooped, raking the uppermost leaves of the trees with his shiny, love-colored hooves. Whirlwinds of seed pods and startled bugs swirled in the wake of his powerful form as he soared through the crystal air.

Prince Dreamshine, with handfuls of the cotton-candy mane of the unicorn, rode upon Fufflemuff's proud back. Dreamshine's elfin face shone a smile in the sunlight, and his luxurious eyelashes protected his startling green eyes from the dusty sugar sprinkles that burst in clouds from Fufflemuff's beating wings. He was shirtless, wearing only leather breeches, and his bare feet caressed the unicorn's velvety hide as they soared.

A glistening sheen of sweat highlighted Dreamshine's per-fectly-muscled body, and tiny bits of magic and butterscotch dreams clung to his flowing blond hair as they dove low over the King's Fields and its hundreds of miles of swaying flowers.

Mount Starstuff, with its cosmic snow peaks, loomed ahead. They flew close, taking in the beauty of the mythical mountain. Miracle streams flashed with smiles, snaking down the southern face in glowing rivulets, runoff from the ghostly, nebula-fogged ridges above. Trees waved and called his name as Dreamshine buzzed the cliffs, keen on spotting any of the careless nymphs who often tanned their pale bodies on the moss-covered crags, believ-ing themselves safe in their unwary nakedness so high in the sky.

The green-haired girls would scream as he flew by on Fuffle-muff, and they would bashfully hurl themselves into the under-brush, ripping up handfuls of roots and vines to cover their sun-kissed flesh. It was Dreamshine's favorite pastime, and when the nymphs could catch him, they would flip their weed-tangled hair in his face and whisper honey-dripping spells in his ears; he would be in their thrall forever. They could not catch him, how-ever.

They could only curse at him and throw rocks from their shady warrens. But they threw like girls, and he laughed and laughed.

Nova-bursts crackled and danced in their passing as Fufflemuff's wings skimmed the tumbling black voids of the star-jeweled waterfalls.

Dreamshine saw something, a glinting flash from below like the pulse from a dying sun, flickering in one of the streams that lazily flowed from the foot of the mountain. It was a metal something-or-other, poked at by sunlight, and whatever it was, it hadn't been there yesterday.

"Something below, friend!" Dreamshine hollered against the scented winds. "Something new!"

Fufflemuff had seen it too, and he spiraled downwards like a leaf until he landed on the white sand bank of the bubbling stream.

Dreamshine leapt from his back, and Fufflemuff angled his large black eyes to see what mystery lay shining. The prince squatted by the stream and dipped his hand into the cool water.

He pulled out a round tube of gray metal with words embossed on the side in striking red. It was small, like a cigar case, and it had a crease in its body that promised an opening. It was feather-light, and nothing shifted inside as Dreamshine turned the tube over in his hands, inspecting it carefully.

The letters on the front of the tin spelled out **Biohazard** in bold script.

"It says 'biohazard,' Fufflemuff." Dreamshine said, his fine features twisting in thought. "What does that mean, I wonder? Should I open it?"

"It looks to be from the world of men, my Prince," Fufflemuff said. "Perhaps you should take it to the King. He'll know what to do with it."

"I can make a decision without the aid of my father!" Dreamshine snapped. He tried to open the tube. Every which way he tinkered with the mysterious item, but he could not figure it out.

The prince looked at the tube for a moment more, then showed it to his friend, who shrugged as best as a unicorn could. Dreamshine snorted dismissively and jumped on Fufflemuff's back.

"We'll throw it at the nymphs!" Dreamshine said, and with a massive blast of beach sand, unicorn wings propelled them skyward to the looming juts of the mount.

Prince Dreamshine flung the shiny tube at the nymphs as they danced around a hastily-constructed effigy of him that burned bright blue in the midday shadows of the foggy bluffs.

The nymphs had wrapped themselves in dead leaf dresses and straps of withered vine, and sweat that smelled of dandelions rolled off their writhing bodies as they jittered in choreographed hate, some ancient woodland protest prayer for the prince's untimely evisceration.

The odd artifact bounced off one of the green-haired heads and the tube tumbled into the mystical fire. It melted quickly and produced a foul odor.

The angry nymphs bounced and railed at Dreamshine as he laughed and rode Fufflemuff high above. They called him several names, including, 'mardruke' and 'tindlespot.' The prince and Fufflemuff flew away, and Mount Starstuff disappeared into the mists of memory, like a child's cry of loneliness.

"What in blazes is a 'mardruke,' Fufflemuff?" the prince asked as they penetrated the soft, wet clouds, Fufflemuff's hard, pink horn leading the way.

"I believe it refers to one who defiles a funeral feast with bodily fluids," Fufflemuff said through a mouthful of cirrus wisps.

"Filthy little trollops," Dreamshine snorted, and they burst in a blurry dash of color from a creeping, moist cloud.

Quivering droplets scattered and dried on Dreamshine's taut, muscular chest as he and Fufflemuff drifted through the caressing rays of the four suns that shone down on Furthest Forest. The unicorn's wings beat a fine mist of cloud moisture that kept the prince glistening in the hot, solar crossfire of the sky.

"Onward, Fufflemuff," he said, his flowing blond hair drying in the warm air. "To the scattered islands of the Black Ocean, my friend, free from the oppressive yoke of the same and the known! Oh, my heart! It clamors for the high adventure of those secret places, and all the mysterious and uncharted lands waiting in the waves!"

"Well, okay," Fufflemuff said worriedly. "But would you at least like to fetch a sword and boots, or perhaps a shirt?"

"High adventure needs no shirt!" Dreamshine rumbled. "It needs only a fine and stout sort, a hearty pair like us to grab it by the throat, and wring excitement like cream from a thundermelon! My shirt is the sky!"

Off they flew into the unknown stretches of the Black Ocean, their minds reeling with mermadic and piratical possibilities, and their hearts whispering silent prayers of protection against the seething behemoths of legend that certainly plotted below in the shadowy depths.

The tree was the tallest and fullest tree Jackson had ever seen, and it provided a perfect vantage point for his high *hide*, which was basically just a hammock and camouflage netting. It had taken him an hour and a half to climb the massive tree, and all the equipment he'd lugged up hadn't helped in the ascent.

He obsessively ran his hands over his green and brown fatigues, checking equipment, and he resisted the urge to count the water and food ration packs that hung on nearby branches in olive bags.

He straightened his helmet again and he leaned forward to peer through his mounted scope. He still couldn't believe he was looking at the golden castle in the distance, even though he'd been watching it for a day. It was an actual castle, a truly golden one, and all kinds of weird people and creatures had been coming and going across the gatehouse drawbridge. Storybook things. Nothing was happening at the castle yet, but he knew it was just a matter of time.

"Payload should have popped its cork by now," Jackson whispered to himself. He turned the scope to check on a few of the many visible villages and towns scattered throughout the wooded vista. Nothing yet. Could be days.

"What's your name?" a tiny, squeaking voice suddenly asked.

Jackson recoiled and gasped in surprise. On top of his scope stood a tiny, blue, naked girl with wings, four inches tall and throwing off sparkling dust. She had her hands on her hips, a sincere smile on her face, and her buzzing wings brought life to her long blue hair. He held his palm out to her. She giggled and hopped onto his outstretched hand. She knelt there in his palm, wings fluttering, and she gazed up into his face with happy curiosity. Jackson frowned. These things, he thought, had no fear of man.

"My name is Twee!" the girl said, or nearly sung.

Jackson closed his hand around her and crushed her to death. He put her tiny corpse into the refuse bag that hung nearby, with the corpses of two other tiny, friendly, winged girls who had introduced themselves to him.

They must have been sprites or pixies or something, he figured. He continued his watch, and hoped that his superiors hadn't lied about the inoculations.

King Lovebubble sat alone in his dimly-lit throne room, brooding. His sharp eyes stared at nothing and his long gray beard lay flopped in his lap. The nine mystical jewels inlaid in his crown sparkled and glowed, sending weak, magic flashes of light skittering across ancient tapestries and rugs. He slumped on his throne, his silence interspersed with periodic huffs and sighs.

The large, golden doors of the throne room creaked open, and in limped Hargoth, the Seer. The robed man, his face hidden in the folds of his hood, shuffled to the foot of the king's throne. He slowly knelt there and bowed his head.

"Where is he, Seer?" Lovebubble growled.

Hargoth's ghostly voice floated up from beneath his shadowed hood. "Your son is headed to the Black Ocean, into danger and the mists beyond."

"That boy," the king said. "I've given that boy everything. He cares nothing for his responsibilities. Always adventure, always excitement; that's all he cares about. That and tormenting the nymphs. And now he defies my law by traveling beyond the borders of the Furthest Forest!" The king stood and raged his fists at the ceiling, his jeweled robes jingling. "It shall not stand! Not for one moment longer! Hargoth! You shall go forth to the lair of Kremtrok the Horror Fairy!"

"Not him, My Liege!" Hargoth shuddered. "Anyone but him!"

"Silence! Command him in my name to venture forth and return my wayward son to me."

Hargoth struggled to his feet and limped from the throne room.

The king plopped back down on his throne and seethed. King Lovebubble treasured his son, secretly wishing that he could be as carefree as his boy, but he fretted the fate of Furthest Forest if the rule over the kingdom ever fell into Dreamshine's hands.

"Don't be too hard on him, Father," came a silky voice from a dark corner of the throne room.

The king was startled for a second and he smiled. "Ah, I forgot you were there, daughter."

Every bit the spirit and image of her sainted mother, Princess Sugarbreeze moved across the golden tiles of the throne room in an effortless glide. Her beauty was unearthly, marble-carved, and her heart and devotion soothed the king in the most trying of times. She wore no crown, needing no proof of her nobility, and she wore a simple azure dress, eschewing ornament and fashion. Her honey-colored hair swayed as she bowed slightly, and through shiny tumbles she fixed her dizzying green eyes on her father. She waited for him to speak.

"What am I to do with him?" he asked.

His face alight with discovery, Prince Dreamshine pointed as hard as he could at a tiny green dot in the dark blue expanse. It was an island. Fufflemuff angled his winged form and they descended. Their three days over the ocean had not been kind to them.

Both the prince's flowing blond hair and Fufflemuff's velvety pink hide were matted with salt spray from the sea, and the two wanderers were perilously close to being addled by the glare of the staring suns and the hypnotic endlessness of the water. The unicorn needed no sleep, but when night fell, the prince slept fitfully mid-flight as they sailed through the starry sky. Below was the first island they had yet seen on their spur-of-the-moment journey.

Fufflemuff landed heavily on a beautiful white beach, legs wobbly, the tips of his wings drooping into the hot sand. Prince Dreamshine slid off his back like a limp dishrag, trudged to the pendulum of the tide, and flopped into the water face-first. Fufflemuff followed, walking into the foamy surf up to his belly. He dipped his head and wings into the water, washing off the grime of the past days.

Refreshed and clean, they lumbered from the sea and surveyed their discovery.

"It's an island, all right," Fufflemuff said as he shook off beads of water.

Dreamshine swept his wet hair from his handsome face and pointed at the wall of jungle that faced them. "An island, yes! And what mysteries lie beyond this veil of..." He stopped suddenly. "You know, I'm actually hungry. I don't remember the last time I was hungry. I'm thirsty, too."

"I could eat," Fufflemuff said. "Do you think there might be apples here?"

"Maybe," Dreamshine said. "Maybe something even better than apples! A fruit unknown!"

"Better than apples? Let's go look!"

They cautiously began to pick their way into the trees and undergrowth. Strange nuts, berries, and an odd fruit or two passed their lips and sated their hunger as they worked through the jungle. Wet, clinging vines slapped at them, and foreign burrs and twigs found purchase in their hair and fur.

Clear, bubbling streams quenched their thirst and gave them a path to follow. The moist shadows slithered with hidden creatures, the weak light that pushed through the dense canopy above glinted off hiding, suspicious eyes, and the humid air swam with unidentifiable insects that harried and buzzed.

But there was something, a song, a distant tune filtering through the cackles of birds, the tiny sound of a flute echoing from beyond the leafy gloom. Dreamshine and Fufflemuff kept going, struggling through the green, floral web, keen on finding the source of the beautiful and mysterious music.

Then they came upon a most curious sight. A black cat sat on a rock in the middle of a clearing. He was the one playing the flute. The rock on which he was sitting was surrounded by little blankets full of trinkets: seashells, fruit, notable driftwood, and scores of shiny gimcracks and gewgaws. A little sign was hung on a pole stuck in the ground. The sign read *Muscalabra Trading Post*.

As Dreamshine and Fufflemuff approached, divesting themselves of jungle twigs and burrs, the black cat continued his song, watching them with yellow eyes. The tune was a beautiful and comforting anomaly in the desolate jungle, a balm that erased fear and uncertainty. They stood before the cat and happily waited for him to finish his wonderful piece.

The black cat set his flute carefully on the rock, and smiled at the new arrivals. "Welcome to Muscalabra Trading Post!" the cat said jovially, waving his paws. "My name is Borfuss, and we have many fine items for your perusal!"

Before Dreamshine could say anything, the cat picked up a seashell and listened intently for several moments, his furry face scrunched up and focused on whatever he heard in the shell. "One moment," he said, then jumped off the rock and turned the sign around. It now read *Groonglematz Trading Post*. "Another corporate takeover, I'm afraid. So, what can I do for you?"

"I'm Prince Dreamshine, son of King Lovebubble of Furthest Forest," he said with a slight bow, "and this is my friend, Fufflemuff. We're honored to meet you, Borfuss."

The cat gave a bow and his whiskers prickled to a smile as he returned to his rock. "Well met, Prince Dreamshine and Fufflemuff. I've heard tales of your father's kingdom, and the honor is mine."

"May I?" the prince asked, gesturing towards the assorted bric-a-brac.

"Please," Borfuss smiled.

The prince looked over the cat's wares carefully, giving the display of goods their proper due. From time to time, Dreamshine would confer silently with Fufflemuff, nodding in agreement at the quality and selection. When the correct time had been spent in perusal, the prince said, "You have a significant and unique collection, Borfuss. However, much to my shame, I find I am unable to buy anything at this time."

The cat waved his paws and shook his head. "No, no. I appreciate your thoughtful and considerate shopping. It's rare to find customers who know the good ways, the old ways. It's the tradition that you miss, the customs. Your father has taught you diplomacy well, Prince Dreamshine."

"Tell that to the nymphs," Fufflemuff mumbled under his breath.

"So, friend Borfuss, would you say that our business has been concluded with satisfaction?" Dreamshine asked.

"Most certainly!" Borfuss smiled. "Let us now speak as friends!"

Dreamshine sat on the ground, and the cat settled comfortably on his rock. Borfuss gestured to the prince, graciously allowing the guest to steer the conversation.

"Friend Borfuss, this is an interesting choice of location for your trading post. Very, ah, picturesque," Dreamshine said.

"And desolate," Fufflemuff added.

"There is that," Dreamshine said.

"I've been in business for six years now, in this faraway place," Borfuss said. "Since I was stranded here long ago. I never expected even one customer, and now I've had two. So, I'd say I'm doing rather well." He smiled.

"What about the sign? The shell?" Dreamshine asked.

"One drawback of such a fine location is that you run the very real risk of going completely mad," the cat said. "Because of the loneliness, you see." Borfuss stared off at nothing.

"And are you completely mad?" Fufflemuff asked.

Borfuss looked at Fufflemuff thoughtfully for a moment. "I'm getting there." He smiled again.

"Well, my friend and I are on a tour of the islands in the Black Ocean," Dreamshine said as he stood up. "Sampling the local color and such. If you were so inclined, we'd be happy to have you along."

"Oh yes, please," Borfuss said.

Hargoth the Seer, after several days of dusty riding, found himself finally near the lair of Kremtrok the Horror Fairy. He hated the beast, and he didn't want to call on him. But the king was the king and Hargoth was not, so there you had it.

He reined his horse in at an overgrown mouth of a cave, hidden unless one knew where to look. He slowly eased himself from his horse, babying his crippled leg.

Leaving the horse to graze in a patch of grass, he limped to the entrance of the Horror Fairy's lair.

"Kremtrok!" Hargoth yelled. "In the name of King Lovebubble of Furthest Forest, I call you forth!"

An angry moan drifted from the darkness, a gravelly rumble of annoyance. Something shifted in the darkness.

"Go away," came a growling sandpaper warning. "I'll eat your eyes!"

"Heed my call, Kremtrok!" Hargoth persisted. "I speak for the King!"

There was another moan and then movement: a scraping of walls, kicking of rocks, some reluctant shuffling. Past the vines that covered the cave's mouth came Kremtrok.

The cursed, mutant fairy was seven feet tall and dressed in rags, with huge folded and twitching batwings hanging from his wide back.

He had coal black skin that bore the raised scar-like runes of a witch's diabolical attention.

His ape-like, brutish face no longer held any remnant of a fairy's beauty, and his burning red eyes shone through the stringy mop of filthy, long hair that framed his face.

The hands at the ends of his overlong arms had clawed fingers that endlessly and slowly wiggled as if they dreamt of murder, and the yellow razors of his teeth ground and snapped around grunts and growls.

Kremtrok lumbered petulantly up to Hargoth and scraped words from the grindstone in his throat. "King has seven favors, then he dies!" the creature said.

Hargoth willed himself in place, not wanting to show weakness by taking a backwards step. "Prince Dreamshine has ventured out onto the Black Ocean. You're to find him and his unicorn, and bring them before the king unharmed."

"The king has six favors," Kremtrok stonily hissed.

"Yes," Hargoth said, sweating under his hood. "After you do this, six favors left."

"Then he dies," the monster growled as he unfurled his leathery wings, joints popping. "And so do you." Kremtrok's powerful legs launched him into the sky, where his wings found the air, and he was gone.

Hargoth breathed a sigh of relief until several naked, feral nymphs burst from the underbrush and began to rip him apart and eat the pieces, overwhelming him in seconds.

He was surprised, in his final thoughts before his life drained from his body, that he hadn't seen it coming.

With, Dreamshine and Borfuss on his back, Fufflemuff soared through the blue skies searching for Kitty Island.

Flocks of strange birds scattered before them, and dark shapes swirled in the murky waters below.

Borfuss was dressed for adventure, wearing a chain-mail tunic secured by a leather belt, from which hung a tiny dagger and his flute.

His little sword was slung across his back. He hung on with both of his front paws, nervously glancing at the water below from time to time.

Dreamshine sported a pair of shiny, red leather buccaneer boots, a gift from Borfuss that the cat had found washed up on the beach years earlier, worn by the bloated corpse of a careless pirate.

The stock of the trading post had been left behind gladly; a move that Borfuss said ushered in a welcome career change. The trio searched for the castaway cat's former home as their eyes scanned the blue horizon.

"You know," Borfuss said smugly, "before I left on my ill-fated expedition, Queen Essodeay had an eye for me. Quite an eye indeed!"

"Is that so?" Dreamshine said.

"It is. I wonder, Prince Dreamshine, is it vain to hope that she might think of me from time to time?" the cat asked.

"Vain?" Dreamshine said. "I think not! In my estimation, you're a very good cat, and if your queen has spent some time pining for you, well…it's time well spent!"

Borfuss beamed as they searched for his island.

Princess Sugarbreeze walked the battlements of Castle Love-bubble, her ornate bow in hand, her quiver of arrows hanging from her left hip.

She wore the plain, gray metal armor of a common soldier, and she walked among a contingent of archers who scanned the surrounding forest with eagle eyes.

She saw movement, hundreds of yards away in the brush, and notched an arrow, drew, and held fast.

She was a stone, still but for her honeyed hair whipping in the wind, as her jade eyes bore into the woodlands, searching for a target. But the things were clever.

She replaced the arrow in the quiver. Her father appeared by her side, clad in his golden armor. Two similarly dressed royal guardsmen stood behind him.

"How many were able to make it inside, Father?" the princess asked, her gaze still scanning.

"A few hundred at most," King Lovebubble said sadly. "Those who aren't safe here behind our walls…well, I fear that most of the kingdom may fall victim to this curse."

"How could it spread so quickly?" Princess Sugarbreeze sighed. "How could we have been taken by such surprise?"

"The time for answers will come, daughter," the king said as he adjusted his golden helmet. "But for now, there is only the castle and our people."

"And Dreamshine?" she asked, turning to look at her father. "What of my brother?"

"I must spare no thought for him, or my heart may break," he said.

"Don't lose hope, Father," she said, searching his face. "He may still be alive."

With a grunt the king turned and continued along the walls of his castle, bolstering his troops with his presence.

Princess Sugarbreeze looked at the faces of the soldiers. Some were scared, some determined, and she loved them all, as well as all of her countrymen who fought with her.

She pretended that she had never seen the golden towers of Castle Lovebubble before, even though she had lived in them all her life, and the beauty of the castle sung to her.

She thought of her mother, waiting in the Otherworld, taken by war so many years ago. And she thought of her older brother, the dreamer, who cared nothing for matters of royal concern. She wished Dreamshine were with her now, because there was an army of dead things out in the forest, and if he were there with her, at least they could die as a family. Her face hardened as she watched the forest.

Suddenly, twenty of the dead things burst from the trees and scattered, making for the castle. They were a loping, motley lot: undead elves, rotted gremlins, even an axe-dragging zombie dwarf.

"Fire at will!" she screamed, and notched her arrow.

The first volley tore into the zig-zagging creatures; their inhuman eyes were lustfully locked onto the living elves manning the walls.

The arrows in their undead bodies were minor annoyances to the slavering, moaning things, but when the shafts found their heads, they finally dropped. Two of them had made it as far as the moat.

Who knew how many crept about in the woods beyond?

Jackson observed the continuing siege through his scope. His refuse bag was full of tiny, colorful corpses. The castle was holding up well, but he figured it wouldn't be much longer till it fell. The dead things crashed into the castle, wave after ravenous wave, breaking and receding only to crash again.

It was an awesome, horrible sight. He scanned his scope, running the lens over the ruined, smoking villages and zombie-choked towns. It was all going according to plan. He wondered how much longer he was going to have to be an eyewitness to the ongoing slaughter—two weeks, three?—before he was relieved.

He caught movement through his scope, far away in the blue sky. He zeroed in on the blurry dot and magnified. It was a dragon.

A red dragon glided among the clouds, giant batwings beating, blood-colored scales sparkling in the light of the multiple suns. Jackson gasped. It was beautiful.

Kremtrok, pressed into service by Dreamshine, who promised to willingly return to Furthest Forest in exchange for the dark fairy's help, advanced on Meowsburg, the capital of Kitty Island. Olt Blasko and his sinister band of Cat Creeps had pulled off a daring coup d'état, dethroning Queen Essodeay and occupying Castle Kitty.

Tiny cannon fired from the castle walls and bad kitties let arrows fly. The projectiles bounced harmlessly off Kremtrok s skin and he laughed, outwardly annoyed that he'd agreed to help the errant prince, but inside secretly joyful that he was set loose to destroy.

Shops and windows slammed their shutters, and mothers grabbed their kittens and ran for cover as the looming fairy stomped ever closer to the cannonball-spitting stronghold. He was a giant anyway, but compared to the cat-sized buildings, Kremtrok was ridiculously huge, like one of the legendary titans of old that once wandered the plains of Furthest Forest, stomping yurts and yaks.

Kremtrok broke into a run, thundering down the main street of Meowsburg like a mobile earthquake, and when he reached the castle he didn't stop. He leapt the moat and threw his mass into the gatehouse, obliterating the structure in an explosion of splintered drawbridge and shattered stone.

Treasonous tabbies and seditious Siamese scattered before him as he roared and shook off the remnants of the gatehouse. Olt

Blasko raged from the walls of the keep, hissing at his soldiers to keep fighting. Kremtrok began to kill them all.

On a hill overlooking Meowsburg, Prince Dreamshine sat in the grass watching the destruction below. Queen Essodeay and Borfuss sat next to him, and the queen's band of supporters milled nearby. Fufflemuff grazed happily, not interested in watching the slaughter.

The queen, her beautiful white fur rippling in the breeze, looked at Dreamshine. "Your friend is most effective," she said. "This rebellion should be quelled within the hour."

"Glad to be of service, Your Majesty," he replied. "We royals have to stick together."

"But are you sure you can't stay for a while, Prince Dreamshine?" Borfuss asked. "What about your tour of the Black Ocean?"

"Cut short, I'm afraid. My father calls from Furthest Forest and his reach is long." He looked at Borfuss. "Besides, if I refused to go home, Kremtrok would simply force me to go."

"But you will come back for a visit?" Essodeay asked. "We'll have a feast waiting in your honor."

"Oh, I'll be back," Dreamshine said. "There are so many more places to explore, and I don't want to miss any of them!"

"Oh look," the queen said. "Your monster just ripped Olt Blasko in half. Well, good riddance!"

Orcs and elves, nymphs and trolls, and a multitude of other creatures great and small—all dead—continued their endless attack on Castle Lovebubble.

The siege dragged on day after day of cunning attacks, of zombified gnomes and undead leprechauns crawling and squeezing through the waterworks, their biting faces popping out of drains, of rotting dwarves tunneling, draining the moat and weakening the walls with their sinkholes, and of grunting trolls chipping away at the walls with their war hammers as they shrugged off arrows.

The fletchers worked around the clock fashioning arrows from table legs, and the remaining soldiers' sword arms felt like lead weights, spent from desperate hacking. The battle raged continuously, and the numbers of the relentless dead continued to grow.

"Our spells roll off their backs like water!" Jim Jim, the Royal Spellcaster, cried at the gathering of officials in the castle's keep. Jim Jim swooned; he was known to be an overly dramatic fop. "I tell you, these creatures aren't cursed! They're under no spell!" He held his fat, sweaty face in his hands and shivered beneath his multicolored robes.

"That's what I've been saying all along!" Dr. Raven yelled, the royal physician. "This is a disease, a sickness!"

King Lovebubble, his golden armor marred and spattered with blood, sat wearily on his throne. His gore-caked sword lay across his lap. "There can be no cure?" he asked Dr. Raven.

"My King," Raven said, bowing his head slightly. "There is no known cure for death. The things outside may walk, but they have no life. The only cure is a sword or an arrow, as we have seen. We must root out and destroy them all, Your Majesty, for if even one remains, the cycle will begin anew!"

"Then that's what we will do," Princess Sugarbreeze growled. "Every last one of them will die!" She sounded surer than she felt. She looked at her father.

The king had taken no rest for days and was fighting on willpower alone, and his heroics were a proud example to the soldiers and civilians defending the castle.

No one, including her, wanted to let him down.

The golden doors to the throne room flew open and a harried soldier ran to the king and knelt. "They've breached the walls, My Lord!"

"Then it's time!" the king said. "I command every man, woman, and child to fight!" He stood and strode powerfully from the room, his well-used armor clanking.

Princess Sugarbreeze walked over to Jim Jim, who cowered in a heap. She pulled the short, heavyset man to his feet and brought his face close to hers. "If your spells don't work, then you pick up a sword!" she hissed, and followed her father outside.

Prince Dreamshine and Fufflemuff, followed closely by Kremtrok, flew over the woodlands of Furthest Forest, horrified by the sight of Castle Lovebubble under siege, the moat drained and the walls breached. Their vantage point provided them with an unobstructed view of the carnage. Hundreds of the denizens of his father's kingdom were streaming into the castle, which was defended by a dwindling number of soldiers and citizens.

"What in blazes?" Dreamshine yelled over the din of battle.

"Ooh, a battle," Kremtrok cooed.

"Let's get down there!" Dreamshine commanded, and Fufflemuff flew towards the stone keep. The prince's heart sank. His sister was cradling the mangled body of their father, who had seemingly been struck down by the massive, hammer-swinging mountain troll that was being held off by a score of desperate soldiers.

Dreamshine leapt from Fufflemuff's back before they'd even landed; he dropped to the ground next to his ruined family. Fufflemuff and Kremtrok landed behind him. Attacks were coming from all sides, and the dead would soon engulf the living.

"Father!" Dreamshine screamed as he fell to his knees next to his sister.

King Lovebubble lived just long enough to see his son returned, then he died.

"What has happened here, sister?" Dreamshine yelled over the crash of fighting all around them. He grabbed her bloodied, armored shoulder and turned her to him.

Princess Sugarbreeze blinked through tears, staring at him in shock for a moment. She looked exhausted. "An army of the dead is attacking, brother, and our brave father is dead."

Dreamshine pulled his sister close and hugged her armored form.

"You're king now, brother," she said into his ear. "King of a doomed kingdom."

Dreamshine stood and walked over to Kremtrok and looked up at his brutish face. "I'm the king now, Kremtrok," he proclaimed with a tear in his eye. "I have a favor to ask you. Destroy these dead things; every last one of them!"

"Five more favors," Kremtrok smiled, "and then you die." He turned, unfurled his wings and flew straight at the mountain troll, then straight through the mountain troll, tearing the creature to twitching pieces. He was swarmed by the undead, but if his hide couldn't be pierced by wood or blade, then teeth had no chance. He thundered forth, popping zombie heads like grapes and crushing them beneath his feet. The soldiers followed him with renewed hope as they annihilated any stragglers left in Kremtrok's wake. Fufflemuff, on his own initiative, took to the sky, his hooves finding the heads of many a careless zombie.

Dreamshine turned to see his sister locked in combat with the corpse of his father.

He rushed to her aid, but needn't have bothered. She wrenched her father's sword from his dead hands and beheaded him in one deft movement.

Then she fell to her knees, her armored chest heaving in cries of sorrow.

Dreamshine helped her up and they entered the keep, Princess Sugarbreeze dragged the king's sword across the stone threshold.

The next few weeks were a blur. Kremtrok, thanks to his uncanny tracking skills and with the aid of Dreamshine and the soldiers, found every last remaining zombie and destroyed them. The new king was absolutely disinterested in all things kingly and abdicated the throne to his sister. Queen Sugarbreeze, with Prince Dreamshine by her side, presided over King Lovebubble's funeral, a solemn and respectful affair.

Dreamshine and Fufflemuff walked through the courtyards of the castle with the queen, surveying the rebuilding of the castle walls. There was an air of newfound hope and optimism in the kingdom of Furthest Forest, and those who had survived the nightmare were just beginning to move on with their lives. Kremtrok had become something of a local hero, less feared than respected, but still kind of feared. He trailed along behind the royal siblings, lumbering next to a still wary Fufflemuff, whose large black eyes kept a careful watch on him.

"I think I shall take my leave of you, sister," Prince Dreamshine said. "I haven't the stomach for these everyday things. I must return to the Black Ocean and adventure." He was properly outfitted this time, with a suit of light armor, his rapier, and his sister's bow and quiver, a gift from her for his coming excursion.

"You won't be gone too long, I hope," Queen Sugarbreeze said, kissing her brother on his cheek.

"Only as long as excitement calls!" He smiled and returned her kiss. "Farewell!"

He walked over to Fufflemuff and leapt onto his pink back.

"Oh good, now you're wearing armor," Fufflemuff grumbled.

"You know," Dreamshine said, smiling at the Horror Fairy. "I like you, Kremtrok. Would you like to come along on our tour of the Black Ocean?"

Kremtrok, who had never been invited by anyone to go anywhere almost felt a tear or two well up in his awful, red eyes "All right," he said, and looked toward the Queen. "Four more favors…"

"Then I die," Queen Sugarbreeze said, smiling.

Dreamshine, Fufflemuff, and Kremtrok flew into the air, aiming for all the mysterious places they could find.

"You do realize that no monarch of Furthest Forest will ever ask you for that last favor," Dreamshine said.

"I know," Kremtrok sighed.

The queen watched them until she could see them no longer in the distance, and then she occupied herself with her royal duties.

At the base of Mount Starstuff, on the white sand beach of one of the miracle streams, a humming filled the air—a strange atmospheric disturbance.

Suddenly a blinding white light exploded and stayed; it was a circle of brilliance that shimmered—a portal.

Black-clad soldiers with automatic weapons rushed through the portal and secured the beach, their rifles trained on the forests beyond the stream.

Hundreds of soldiers marched out of the portal next, followed by all-terrain vehicles, armored half-tracks and tanks. Riding in the gunner's position of the last tank was a gruff, gray-haired soldier, chomping on a cigar.

When the tank cleared the portal the circle of light blinked out.

The man with the cigar climbed down out of the tank and surveyed the area as he adjusted the sidearm that was holstered on his right thigh.

"Reynolds!" the man shouted through a cloud of cigar smoke.

From one of the half-tracks came a mousy man, a civilian, dressed as a soldier but his demeanor screamed for a lab coat. He carried a device and scanned the area with it.

"Parts per million…zero point zero one, Colonel. It's safe."

"Think the toxin did its job, son?" the colonel asked.

"The recon unit says that the local population has been severely weakened by the effects of the toxin, sir. Half-life is four weeks, so we shouldn't have to worry about any, uh… zombies."

"Naw, just the elves, trolls, wizards, dragons, and fuckin' fairies!" the colonel growled. "I'm sure this mission'll be a cakewalk!"

A young soldier ran up to the colonel. "Sir! The techs are setting up the command post, Recon Alpha and Gamma are probing out, and Delta are constructing the drones, sir!"

"Very good, Captain," the colonel said. "See to communications, and make sure we have sniper over-watch in position."

"Sir, yes sir!" the captain said, and was off to execute his orders.

A flock of birds unlike anything the colonel had ever seen passed above, a moving cloud of stark beauty. Their calls sounded like musical instruments, blissfully serene.

"I hate this fucking job, Reynolds," the colonel said. He dropped his cigar in the sand and crushed it under his boot heel.

MISSING OBLIVION

ROBERT DUBUQUE

To be able to sleep without fear was a rare thing these days. And I mean really fall into an uninterrupted deep sleep, not just lose half consciousness for a short while. Tonight was a rare occasion. I stumbled on a farm on the outskirts of my father's domain and quickly cleared it. I know there are no wandering dead, and no survivors had claimed the barn as their stronghold. The loft was the most defensible part of the dilapidated structure, so I climbed up there to make a bed. At least for tonight, I would dream.

My body felt as if it was going to collapse before I could even get myself settled. I unslung my crossbow and laid down my quiver next to it. I removed my belt and kept my short sword within arm's reach. My arms barely had the strength to remove my coat so I could use it as a pillow.

The last thing that went through my mind before sleep closed my heavy eyelids was that I should never be tired again after sleeping for a hundred years.

I dreamed of my first days awake in the new kingdom.

Though it has been years since I woke up from my century long slumber, I can still remember my first moments of consciousness perfectly. Fittingly enough, the first thing I saw was terrifying.

A man was bent over me, just pulling back from kissing my lips. The first thing I noticed about him was the smell. His stale breath pervaded my nostrils, and he had the unpleasant odor of a beggar. I slapped him across the face.

He backed away with a look of shock in his eyes, holding the side of his face that I'd slapped. "I realize I don't look like royalty, but I think a little gratitude is in order for breaking the witch's curse!" he exclaimed, clearly insulted.

"What are you talking about? Where are my guards and how did you get in here?" I demanded, taking in my surroundings. I looked around the room I was in, still groggy from sleep.

I was clearly at the top of one of the castle's towers, in the center of a bare stone-walled room. There was a single glassless window to my right, directly across from the door the oaf had broken in.

The oaf was just staring at me, a look of sadness in his eyes. This was the first time I'd really observed him. He was undoubtedly gaunt, despite the fact that his face was covered by a thick growth of beard. His long, unwashed hair hung over his shoulders. His clothes were dirty and his sword looked well used. He was decidedly unfit to be in my father's castle.

"You've been asleep a long time, Princess. I apologize for my appearance, but if you would but look out the window, you may excuse it," he replied, clearly reciting something he'd rehearsed before. He gestured toward the window.

I got out of the small bed in the center of the circular room. On unsteady feet, I approached the window. As with the oaf, the first thing that shocked me upon nearing the window was a terrible odor. It smelled like a butcher's shop in an open air market during the summer.

My eyes were nearly overflowing with tears as I took in my father's fallen kingdom. The crumbled remains of the castle were being overtaken by weeds, and the moat surrounding my beautiful home was dry. I could see the courtyard, once the envy of other kingdoms throughout the land, was now full of the same weeds that were reclaiming my family's castle.

I turned to the scruffy man that had brought me into this nightmare and could barely form the words to ask him what had happened. He sat down heavily on my bed and patted the spot next to him. In a trance, I walked over and took the offered seat. He turned to me and began his tale in a tone of sadness no bard has ever matched.

"Before you went to sleep, Princess, your father's kingdom was a shining beacon of hope for the future. As you know, your people worshipped your father, and your father's love for you was second to none. The only darkness in your kingdom came in the form of an ancient and jealous witch. Knowing that it would break the great king's heart, she cursed you to eternal slumber; a veil of sadness and unrest fell over the kingdom when you were cursed."

He put his hand on mine and looked into my eyes.

"Your father's love for you was so great that he took ill when you were cursed. His conniving brother seized his chance at the throne, and began wooing your mother, the queen, before the king had even passed. The new king, now married to the queen, attempted to win over the hearts of his people with daring and expensive quests. His knights traveled the land, slaying dragons and taming unicorns, all for the glory of the kingdom.

"It was working. The people were warming to the new king, but he desired their undying loyalty so much, that he mounted a dangerous and impossible quest: to murder the sorceress that had cursed his niece. But he failed. The witch was so angry at the attempt on her life that she ordered the hungry dead to rise. Across the land, graveyard soils were unturned, and hordes of corpses shambled throughout your father's kingdom, infecting the people with their insatiable appetite for flesh."

He stood up and walked towards the window, turning his back to me.

"It has been a full century since you went to sleep, Princess, and order can never be restored. There are no strongholds against these undead villains. The only way to survive is to keep moving, stay quiet, and kill only when necessary."

I was shocked. I wouldn't have believed this man had I not looked upon my father's castle and seen the devastation for myself. "How did you find me?" I asked, with more questions lining up in my head.

"The stories of a sleeping princess have survived the curse of the hungry corpses, and I made it my mission to find you. I've been very lonely these last years," he said, with just a hint of shame in his eyes.

"You woke me up into what you describe as a cold, nightmarish existence because you wanted *company*?" I asked as I rose, an overwhelming feeling of anger welling up in my chest.

He looked at me, clearly outraged that I would be so ungrateful.

"You would prefer to sleep until this tower crumbles to the ground?" he asked.

At the time, I thought this to be a valid point. "So, what's your plan now?" I asked, resigning myself to his company.

As we descended the tower, this man who claimed to be a prince told me of the fall of his own kingdom to the wretched corpses, and explained to me how he had survived.

"You must remember," he said, once again seeming to recite something he'd either said or thought many times, "that hunting the corpses is a foolproof way to get yourself killed. At first, I wanted to slay as many as possible. But they are loud when they fight, and their moans can be heard for miles around. Fighting merely attracts more of them, and my only advantage is speed and intelligence."

When we reached the bottom of the tower, he insisted on exploring the castle in search of weapons or preserved food. I argued with him, for the idea of stealing from my family's palatial home was akin to raiding a tomb in my mind.

"Princess, there are few places that haven't been scavenged by other survivors," he said, "but this place looks relatively untouched. You'll quickly find out in this new land that you must take what you can when it's available. There are no new swords being made. No crops are being grown. There hasn't been a harvest in nearly a hundred years. Scavenging from the old kingdoms is the only way the few survivors can go on."

I agreed to scavenge the castle on the condition that the family's treasury remain untouched. He laughed and told me the riches of the old world were less valuable than a pitcher of water.

We set course for the armory. It was when we were walking down an expansive and crumbling hallway that he shot his arm out and signaled for me to stay quiet. I listened.

Clearly, whatever had him startled hadn't registered with me at first, but then I heard it. A solitary footstep followed by a dragging sound. We stood still and listened as the sound grew closer, coming from a hall in front and to the left of us. He drew his bow and readied an arrow, remaining completely silent. He let fly before the figure turned the corner.

The timing was perfect. In the fraction of an instant that it took the arrow to close the distance between us and the corner, someone just barely stuck their head into the hallway we were occupying. The arrow went directly through the side of the figure's head.

I stifled a scream and sprinted over to the corner. Once again, my nose was keener than my eyes. Although that foreign, rotting meat smell pervaded the castle, the corpse before me wore it like a cloak.

When I got closer, I was astonished that this man was walking at all. One foot was clad in the ancient remains of a hard shoe, but the other foot looked as if it had been ground away to a diagonal, bloody stump. The dead man's clothes hung off him as though there were nothing underneath.

I realized then why the word 'mottled' is rarely used to reference something other than a corpse, for that was the only way to describe the particular shade of green the dead man's skin had taken on. His eyes were a dull yellow, bulging out of the eye sockets of his ruined head.

"Don't dwell on him, Princess, for he's been dead for many years," my rescuer said as he approached me.

I wiped the tears from my eyes and lead him to the armory. He warned me to speak in whispers on the way.

"I assume you smelled the stench that came off of that thing," he whispered as we walked, "but they can smell us even quicker. At all times you must be wary of them, for they'll smell you before you even see them. If there are more in this castle, they already know we're here. Fortunately, we won't be long."

The armory was gone. The doors, which were made of solid oak and as well-guarded as my father's throne room, were in shambles, smashed in and laying on the floor. The weeds were growing between the stones and reclaiming the splinters of the ruined portal.

"Damn," he whispered when he saw the utter emptiness of the large armory, "was there anywhere else weapons were kept?"

"Yes," I replied, "behind the quartermaster's partition there was a secret trapdoor. The hunting weapons of the royal family were kept there. I used to hunt foxes with my crossbow."

We crossed through the crumbling stone arches of the evacuated armory to a caged-in corner. The metal cage fell away without much resistance. Inside of the small room there was a heavy oak table, and when we pushed it out of the way, it revealed a trap door.

I pulled it up and started to descend, but my new companion chivalrously insisted on going down first. I didn't argue. The royal armory was no larger than a common pantry, so despite the lack of light, I could see it was left untouched.

The importance of scavenging was really driven home to me by the rough-looking prince's face. The failing light did little to mask his nearly overflowing eyes when he gazed upon the remnant of the old world.

"I was born into the land of the dead, and in all my years I've never seen something so untouched by the gruesome world we live in," he said softly. "I owe this joy to you, Princess, and you will know soon enough what a rare treasure we've found."

After his speech, he unabashedly stripped out of his old clothes. If we had a torch, he would have seen my cheeks turn red at the sight of his half-nude figure. He turned and smiled.

"That dress is lovely, but you should change into the gear left here for hunting," he said as he put on a thick tunic.

He helped to outfit me with more appropriate clothing. My figure was now hidden by a man's hunting attire. He told me to take a dagger and a short sword, and the crossbow if I was confident with it. His old weapons were left on the floor of the secret armory as he traded up to less-worn pieces.

"We're blessed that this room remained dry after all these years, or these weapons would be useless rust. Now remember, fair maiden, that these weapons are a last resort only. I've managed to live this long through the use of stealth and aversion. A well-aimed head shot is the only thing to take down our enemies, but if they spot you, they'll bring others. Do as I say and follow my rules, and I promise to defend you to my last breath."

As I looked at him and saw the resolve in his eyes, I knew he would keep his word.

The prince kept me safe for years. Over months of trial without error, I learned the rules of survival. Stay quiet. Always have an escape plan. Avoid other survivors, for they are more dangerous than the walking dead when it comes to young women.

I learned quickly. I did things I didn't believe I was capable of. Our day to day existence was filled with fear and whispered conversations. There was one rule I learned that the prince had overlooked, however. Cherish fleeting joys when they came.

Happiness in this dark new world came in the form of a safe place to sleep or an unspoiled tree bearing fruit. On very rare occasions, when we found an easily defended camp, we would even risk a fire and fresh meat. I came to enjoy freshly killed venison more than I had ever savored a feast in my father's kingdom.

I also learned the value of companionship. We were an unlikely duo, and he was much older than I. Despite some less than subtle hints from me, the prince never pursued me romantically. I believe he was the only man left to have such self-restraint, and after his passing, I loved him that much more for it.

He died defending me. We were overwhelmed after a careless afternoon in an apple orchard, where we spent more time in conversation than listening for trouble. A group of scoundrels, the first survivors we'd seen in months, attacked us. It was clear they were after my body and our few belongings, and they did not need the prince alive.

The prince fought valiantly and told me to run, the implication being that he would find me. He knew he would die, and part of me was sure of his demise as well. So I ran.

Tracking other creatures and inferring the demise of survivors was a skill the prince had taught me. When I returned to that orchard a few days later, I found his body, stabbed and ruined. They had taken everything from him, even his boots. My weapons and the small bag of survival tools I'd had when I fled the attackers were all I had left.

I mourned over his body, and took solace in the fact that he'd taken nearly the entire pack of scoundrels with him. That's what they were: a pack. Only wolves can show such disregard for life when it comes to their own primal needs. I also noted that the dead fiends had been stripped naked by their surviving friends. Loyalty and respect were apparently not in their character.

My mourning didn't end with my lost friend. While I was bent over his body in the orchard, I also wept for the world I'd lived in before my century of oblivion, a place where men were brought to justice for their atrocities. I wept for this new land as well, where the evil of the walking dead still didn't rival the evil of a desperate man.

The days were longer without someone to talk to. I moved on without my prince. I scavenged when I had to, but the fleeting joys were fewer and further between. I kept him in my heart at all times, and remembered his wise words. When faced with a decision, I asked myself what he would do, and followed his advice. He never failed me.

I moved south at all times after his death. He always dismissed my idea of moving south, because he claimed the dead moved slower in the cold. He was right about that, but like my mentor, I remembered tales from my childhood. I remembered a traveler who had entered my father's court and told tales of the evil sorceress who would curse his kingdom one day.

The traveler claimed the witch lived in the south, in the warm jungles on the coast. The prince always told me that she couldn't be killed. Whenever I brought up the idea, he would remind me that the dead only walk because of the attempt on her life. He claimed that another attempt would merely incite further horrors on the remaining survivors. I heeded all his lessons after his death except for one. My prince, my protector, was the last bastion of chivalry and selflessness left in this harsh, unforgiving landscape of ravenous corpses and evil men. I had no sympathy for the remaining living, and if my attempt ended the lives of the pathetic few survivors left, then so be it.

I woke up in the barn, the last tendrils of my dream reverie stubbornly clinging to my slowly-waking mind. It was still dark and I was still weary, but there must have been a reason why I had been woken up. I held my breath, listening for any indication that I wasn't alone.

After a few moments, I heard the source of my awakening; the shambling footsteps of a few corpses below me, in the main part of the barn. I had broken one of the prince's cardinal rules: always have an escape plan.

My weapons were useless. If my smell had attracted the three shambling fiends below me, than there could have been an untold number of them waiting just outside the barn, tempted by the scent of a human.

Whenever I was in a position like the one I now found myself in, it was of vital importance that I moved maddeningly slow. Any sound would alert them to my presence, then they would begin their horrid moaning, something akin to a dinner bell in their rudimentary form of communication.

Very carefully, I attached my weapons to myself and slung my pack over my shoulders. I crept over to one of the many holes in the walls of the loft of the barn and peered through to see what I was up against.

There was a horde outside. As far as I could see, corpses were gathering around the barn, aimlessly wandering into each other. My smell on the wind must have attracted an entire mass of them to me. Fortunately, only three had wandered into the barn before I woke up.

While gazing upon the sea of the hungry dead, I looked for any hint of safe passage through the crowd. There were a few weak spots, but nothing ideal. It was just a matter of time before I made too much noise and they swarmed in, either taking down the ancient supports in the barn, or leaving me cowering and stranded in the loft.

I quietly laid out three arrows on the edge of the overhang. I fit the first one into my crossbow and decided in which order it was wisest to dispose of the corpses, based on their line of vision, distance from my bow, and any quick escape I may have needed in case of an inaccurate shot.

I lined up my shot and let the first arrow loose. I knew it was a kill shot as it left my bow, and I started cocking the next arrow while it flew.

The second arrow found its target with the same accuracy, and the third was destroyed before it even reacted to the noise of the first body hitting the ground. The prince would have been proud.

After silently descending from my loft, I moved to the barn door on my toes without making a sound. I caught my breath before sprinting out into the grasping hands that were hungry for live meat.

The crowd seemed endless at ground level. As I sprinted towards my plotted path, a moan rose from the first one that spotted me. The horrible moan was a mixture of pain and hunger, and a sick kind of excitement rippled through the horde like the cheers and groans of gamblers at a jousting match.

My dagger was in my right hand as I sprinted through the crowd, swiftly stabbing through eyes and skulls when I had to, ducking and avoiding when I could. My speed and reaction time couldn't be matched by the starving wretches, but I had to reach the end of the crowded horde soon, or my endurance would give way to weary muscles.

The smell of the decomposing corpses overpowered me and made it difficult to breathe and keep up the speed necessary to survive. If I didn't get through the horde in the next few minutes, I would succumb to the demands of my lungs and heart; I would have to slow down.

I reached the end. I kept up the sprint without looking back for as long as possible, then slowed to a jog before finally glancing over my shoulder. I'd outpaced them by roughly a hundred meters, but the crowd was still moving toward me, the smell of my sweat spurring their appetites.

I jogged for the rest of the night, stopping to drink from my deer skin canteen when I had to. The horde was still following me, but they were barely visible after a few hours.

The plague of the walking dead had one more advantage over me that I was more scared of than anything—they never grew tired. They didn't eat for sustenance, but ate to spread the witch's curse. Water was of no use to them either. They would pursue me and wouldn't stop until they lost my scent.

So I ran.

In this new land, the thing I needed most, the thing that every last survivor wished for, was rest.

Day after day they came after me, while I kept chasing the legend of the witch's lair to the south.

But at the end of each day, I felt so tired that I could sleep for a century.

A VERY BAD DAY IN
FAIRY TALE LAND

ANTHONY GIANGREGORIO

Mr. Wolfe strolled down the winding road through the woods to the large oak tree at the end of the lane.

The oak tree had been in fairy tale land for as long as anyone could remember. On the tree, about waist height, was a small punch clock, and to the side of it were the punch cards for each character in fairyland.

Here, each character would punch in before and after their shift before going off to their prospective places in fairyland. Then they would act out the fairy tale they were part of. Did this seem monotonous? Perhaps, but everyone in fairy tale land had been doing this for so long that no one remembered if there was anything else.

Wolfe looked around the area to see that not many of his friends had punched in to work yet. The woods were normally bursting with life, but today it was positively empty. Was it a holiday and he didn't know?

He heard what sounded like a scream from far away but it was gone before he knew for sure. He simply shrugged, assuming it was a loon or something similar. Maybe it was those damn black ravens that talked like they were from Harlem, he thought.

He saw that the *Three Little Pigs* had punched in but then he assumed they would. Today he was to play the Big Bad Wolf in the tale of the *Three Little Pigs*. He liked that one, for if he got lucky and actually managed to blow the cement house down, he would then get to the choice morsel within the place, namely, the little pig. It hadn't happened yet but he had a good feeling about this morning.

"The one thousand and thirty fourth is the charm," he said to himself as he took his card, punched it, then replaced it in its slot.

He looked up to see Red Riding Hood coming down the road. Her hood was covering her face so he couldn't see her clearly. Her red cloak did look particularly bright this morning, as if it was glistening with wetness, but he didn't give this much thought either. (Being a wolf, he didn't give thought to much of anything usually. He was a blue-collar shmuck in the fairy tale land ranking. He did his job without argument and then rewarded himself for a good day's work by going to the pub for a pint of ale.)

"Hey, Red, what's shakin'?" Wolfe asked as the girl got closer.

Now that Wolfe saw her better, she did seem to have something wet on her, but what was odd was that the liquid was the same color as her bright-red cloak.

Red Riding Hood said nothing as she approached Wolfe, but her arms did rise higher so that she looked like she wanted to give him a hug.

"Whoa, Red, we talked about this," he said. "You and me can't be anything more than friends as long as we're working together."

Red growled low in her throat and Wolfe took this to be a sign of her disproval.

"Listen, Red, that night we spent together was awesome. You did things to me I never even heard of…hell, I probably don't want to hear of them again. But we work together; a relationship will only complicate things." That was when he noticed that Red wasn't acting right. There was something *off* about her, though he couldn't put his paw on it. She did look paler than usual. "Hey, girl, are you all right? You don't look so good."

In reply, she snarled and tried to jump on him, her mouth open and closing as her teeth clacked loudly. But Wolfe was almost double her size so he didn't feel intimidated. He just thought she was trying to be flirty.

"Hey, Red, cut it out. We can't do that here, people will see." He sighed, as if giving in to her urges. "Maybe tomorrow night after our gig with your grandmother. But today I'm working with the Three Little Pigs."

But Red Riding Hood wouldn't stop and she tried over and over to bite him, to rake him with her fingernails. Wolfe pushed her away and she fell back onto her butt. That was when her hood came completely off and Wolfe got a better look at her.

Red Riding Hood's complexion was white as a sheet and she had a large hole in the side of her neck, the blood still seeping from it in small spurts. The wound glistened in the morning light, and Wolfe realized he could see right into her neck. The wound should have been fatal, as there was no way someone could have survived it. Then he saw that she was covered in blood, a lot of it, and no doubt it was her blood.

Jumping to her feet, Red hissed loudly, bared her teeth, and came at Wolfe again. Once more he shoved her away but that time she almost managed to take a bite out of him.

"Red, what's wrong with you? You need to stop this before I get mad."

Ignoring him, Red came at him again, then dodged his sweeping claws and went in to take a bite out of his leg. He jumped back in the nick of time, and out of instinct, kicked out with his foot.

The claw on the big toe on his right foot went right into Red's eye, and it was long enough to pierce her brain.

"Oh shit, I knew I should have cut my toenails." People had been telling him for months but he liked the way his toenails clacked on the sidewalk as he went for a stroll sometimes. Now he'd really done it. He'd killed Red.

No one would believe that a wolf could kill Red Riding Hood by accident, either.

Looking around quickly, he was now glad the area was empty. Picking Red's body up, he carried her deeper into the woods, found a good place, and buried her. His claws made digging easy. He looked like a dog hiding a bone. When he was finished and she was in her grave, he sighed heavily and went back to the punch clock to see if there was any evidence of the murder. There was none, luckily, and the few spots of blood on the grass wouldn't even be noticed by anyone coming to punch in for work.

He knew he needed to act normal, so though he was shook up by everything that had happened, he decided he needed to go to work like always to make sure no suspicion fell on him when it was discovered that Red Riding Hood was missing.

He headed off to the Three Little Pig's neighborhood to begin his day.

By the time he reached the Three Little Pigs' neighborhood, he was feeling much better. Sure he was sad about Red, but then again, he was a wolf after all and wolves killed things. Maybe he was getting soft here in fairy tale land. But then again, being out in the wild was no bowl of cherries. Hunters would try to kill him, and he had to scavenge for food daily. Here he had three squares a day and a job.

The pigs' homes were all lined up on a small cul-de-sac near the edge of town. The closest was made of straw, the next one wood, and the last one of brick.

Going to the straw house, he stood before the door and pulled himself up to his full height. "Okay, let's do this," he mumbled, psyching himself up, then he knocked on the door and said, "Little pig, little pig, let me come in."

He listened for the reply of, "No, not, by the hair of my chinny chin chin." But it didn't come. Instead all he heard was this weird moaning sound from the other side of the door. Scratching his head, he said once more, "Little pig, little pig, let me come in."

Still only moaning, then the sound of something being knocked over.

"What the hell is going on with everyone today?" Wolfe said as he stared at the door. Deciding he might as well just keep up his end of the script, he said in a loud, booming voice, "Then I'll huff and I'll puff, and I'll blow your house in!"

He was about to begin huffing and puffing when the door to the straw house slammed open to reveal the pig standing there, drooling and snarling. His pink complexion was now a dull white and his eyes were void of color. Before Wolfe could yell at the pig for being out of character, the pig lunged for Wolfe, its snout trying to dig a hole in Wolfe's stomach.

Growling angrily, Wolfe slapped the pig away, and before he could stop himself, he pounced on the pig and began to eat it. But as soon as he took a bite he spit it out. "Yuck, this tastes awful."

It tasted like spoiled meat. The pig squirmed beneath him so Wolfe slashed the pig's throat, but when the pig still didn't die, he tore off the little piggy's head and tossed it to the side. It rolled a few feet like a misshapen bowling ball before coming to a halt under the small kitchen table, though the eyes and mouth of the pig continued to move about.

Getting up, Wolfe wiped the blood from his fur, angry at how the situation had played out. After a few minutes he was calm enough to think clearly and he decided he should just keep going on to the next house.

Just for good measure, he blew the straw house down and headed to the next one, this one made of wood.

He knocked on the door and said, "Little pig, little pig, let me come in."

Once more there was no response of, "No, not, by the hair of my chinny chin chin." Instead there was more moaning and groaning.

The Wolfe slapped his face with his right paw and ran the palm over his visage in frustration. "Look, pal, this day isn't going to well for me, so cut it out with the moaning and groaning and get with the program," he said through the closed door to the pig. "Now, you tell me I can't come in and I reply with 'Then I'll huff and I'll puff, and I'll blow your house in!' Then I'll do just that and eat you. I know it sucks but we all have to play our part."

Only moaning came back through the door.

"Fine, have it your way," Wolfe said and he huffed and he puffed and he puffed some more, and at last blew the wooden house down, then though he tried to eat the second little pig, too, this one also tasted terrible so he left the carcass and moved on to the third and last house.

He hated the last house, things never went well for him there. If he did things the way he was supposed to then he was going to end up in a pot of boiling water and the last pig would end up eating him instead of the other way around.

See, when he realized he couldn't blow down a house made of brick, he and the pig were supposed to banter as Wolfe tried to trick him to come out. He would tell the pig that there was a nice field of turnips to be harvested, and when the pig sneaked out alone, tricking him, Wolfe would then tell the pig about a tree with juicy apples in it. Wolfe would then invite the pig to go with him and then of course once outside, the pig would get eaten.

But the pig always got out and returned to the house without Wolfe so he would then tell the pig about a State Fair and would ask if the pig wanted to join him the next day. But the pig would go to the fair alone and buy a butter churn, and when Wolfe arrived the next day, the pig would see the wolf and hide in the churn, but it always fell over and rolled down the hill. Wolfe would see this, get scared and run away. Wolfe never understood why he did that part but he always did what was in the script.

Finally, the pig would laugh at Wolfe and at how he ran away from the butter churn. Wolfe, now angry, was supposed to tell the pig that he was going up to the chimney and then slide down it to get at the pig and eat him that way.

But the pig was clever, and when he saw what Wolfe was about to do, he would hang a large pot full of water in the fireplace, make a blazing fire, and just as Wolfe was coming down the chimney the pig would take off the cover of the pot and Wolfe would fall in. Then the Pig would put on the cover again in an instant, boil the wolf, and eat him for supper. The pig lived happily ever after, too.

But Wolfe decided this time things were going to be different. If the other two pigs could break off from the script, so could he.

The brick house had windows of course and Wolfe had always been angry that he had to go through the chimney when all he had to do was go through a window to get at the pig. But then, he hadn't written the fairy tale and had to play his part the way it was written. Well, not today.

With a mighty leap, he jumped through the window that was to the right of the door, crashing into the house and rolling across the floor with a spray of glass all around him. But there were no squeals of terror from the pig like he expected.

Instead, he found himself facing another blood-thirsty swine, this one holding a butcher's knife with both hooves.

"Right, let's do this," Wolfe said as he got to his feet. Towering over the pig, he wasn't worried about the outcome, even though the pig had a knife.

With a hiss, the pig came at him, and Wolfe dodged to the right, then slashed downward with his claws. The pig was all but cut in half, the two parts peeling from one another like sagging wallpaper. The slice had gone right to the pig's waist, and as the two parts separated, spraying blood in all directions, the legs kept moving. The pig ran across the floor and only stopped upon hitting the far wall with a wet splat before falling over.

Wolfe went to the fallen pig and sniffed the carcass, then turned up his nose at the smell of rotting meat.

"That's it, I'm knocking off early for today. I swear, this is the weirdest day of my life. And that says a lot considering where I live."

So scratching his head once more, and still not putting it all to-gether, he went back and punched out.

"I need a drink…and bad," he said and began walking down the street.

His destination was the pub in the center of town. As he walked there, once again he wondered why the streets were so deserted.

"Wait a second, is that blood over there on the sidewalk?" he wondered as he passed a dark-red stain. He sniffed the air and yes, it sure smelled like blood. Then he passed a bus bench that sure looked like it had brain matter on it, though where the brains had come from was unknown.

This made him want to reach the pub even more. Maybe when he arrived and told his friends what had been going on all day, hopefully they would be able to shed some light on everything. After spotting more blood and gore here and there on the streets and on the lawns of the houses he passed, he decided it must have something to do with Halloween.

"People must be starting early this year," he figured.

Smacking his mouth, he thought ahead to when he was going to get to drink that first beer. He was looking forward to getting the taste of rotten pig flesh out of his mouth.

Upon reaching the pub, he entered and said to all the other customers, "You'll never believe the bad day I've had, guys."

"Wanna bet?" the bartender replied as he sat tied to a chair in the corner of the pub, looking like he was about to become someone's next meal. Which he already was because *Three Blind Mice* were chomping on the bartender's toes, fingers, and one was gnawing on the man's left ear.

The pub was packed and every single patron turned to face Wolfe together.

They were all there. Prince Charming, Beast, Cinderella, Bell, the Ogre under the bridge, Rumplestiltskin, the seven dwarves (though Wolfe only counted six of them in passing, the last one nowhere to be seen), Snow White, Hansel and Gretel, Rapunzel, and many other fairy tale characters.

They all looked terrible, and in fact, Wolfe thought they looked just like Red Riding Hood had. Each one had pale complexions and more than one was covered in blood or had large bite marks on their bodies.

A few were eating something similar to a turkey leg, and from first glance, Wolfe thought the food looked like human arms and legs, though smaller than a normal-size human.

That was when he spotted the limbless torso of the seventh dwarf in a corner of the pub, the body soaked in blood, the dead face wearing a look of terror—the dwarf had been dismembered alive it appeared.

"What's going on here? Hey, why are you guys all looking at me like that?" Wolfe asked as he took a step backwards to the now closed door, thanks to Pinocchio sneaking around behind him and closing it.

"Lunch," Prince Charming said as he got up from his stool; all around him the other zombie characters rose with him, a look of ravenous hunger on their faces.

Moments later, from within the pub, came the death howls of Mr. Wolfe. The screams echoed through the empty streets.

They went on for quite a while.

ABOUT THE WRITERS

Mariah Deitrick is a wife, mother of four, and writer. She's a graduate from the Institute of Children's Literature, and is the author of the adult novel, "Deadly Hunt," and the Young adult novel, "The Forgotten." Her work has appeared in a variety of markets including, Spaceports, Undead Press, and Spidersilk, Knowownder!, Super Teacher Worksheets, Stories That Lift, StoryTeller Tymes, and Living Dead Press.

A complete list of her work can be found at her website www.mariahdeitrick.weebly.com

Robert DuBuque lives in Massachusetts with his wife and daughter. He enjoys reading, writing, and mentally preparing for the apocalypse. When he's not writing he works as a mechanic and hangs out with his little girl.

Anthony Giangregorio is the author of 48 novels and children's books, almost all of them about zombies, and has edited over 40 anthologies and books.

His work has appeared in Dead Science & Metahumans vs. the Undead by Coscom entertainment, Dead Worlds: Undead Stories Volumes 1-7, and Wolves of War by Library of the Living Dead Press. He also has stories in End of Days: An Apocalyptic Anthology Vol. 1-5, the Book of the Dead series Vol. 1-6 by LDP, Zombie Zoology by Severed Press, and two anthologies with Pill Hill Press.

He's also the creator of the 10 book action/zombie series titled "Deadwater" and the apocalyptic series "Warriors of the Apocalypse." His action/horror novel "Dead Rage" is being optioned for a movie at this time.

Meagan Jeffrey is a mother of four beautiful children, who reside in Cambridge Ontario Canada. Meagan started writing in grade 2 when she wrote her first short story that won an Alberta wide short story competition for school aged children. From there, Meagan wrote poetry and won many contests, moved to writing short stories for magazines, short zombie stories that have been published with Living dead press and most recently a novel about Marilyn Monroe that she is hoping to get published.

Shane Koch writes for fun. He lives in Indianapolis. He draws a little too.

R P Steeves is a former teacher and a writer who specializes in the fantastic. His most recent novel, an urban fantasy tale of paranormal detection, "The National Maul" is now available in print and ebook formats, and is the second book in the Misty Johnson series.

Follow his blog and learn of his upcoming horror, fantasy, sci-fi and pulp adventure titles at http://www.rpsteeves.com

Anthony Alexander Valade is an independent horror writer working out of Winnipeg, Manitoba Canada. He has had several poetic works published in a Zombie Anthology titled "Undead Tales 2." Check out his rich and psychedelic "Zombie Poetry" and short stories on Facebook at: ADiethylamide.

UNDEAD PRESS

Where the Dead
Never Sleep

UNDEADPRESS.COM

ZOMBIES, MONSTERS, CREATURES OF THE NIGHT

OPEN CASKET PRESS

OPEN CASKET PRESS.COM
THE NEW NAME IN HORROR

VICTORY OF THE DEAD

ANTHONY GIANGREGORIO

CLAN OF THE BIGFOOT

ANTHONY GIANGREGORIO

RAT WAR

A HORROR ANTHOLOGY

EDITED BY
ANTHONY GIANGREGORIO